MISSISSIPPI
13 GHOSTS
and Jeffrey

MISSISSIPPI 13 GHOSTS and Jeffrey

COMMEMORATIVE EDITION

Kathryn Tucker Windham

With a New Afterword by
Dilcy Windham Hilley and Ben Windham

THE UNIVERSITY OF ALABAMA PRESS
Tuscaloosa

The University of Alabama Press
Tuscaloosa, Alabama 35487-0380
uapress.ua.edu

Hardcover edition published 2015.
Paperback edition published 2021.
eBook edition published 2015.

Inquiries about reproducing material from this work should be
addressed to the University of Alabama Press.

Typeface: Times New Roman

Photographs by Kathryn Tucker Windham (unless otherwise indicated)
Illustrations and cover by H. R. Russell

Paperback ISBN: 978-0-8173-6047-4

A previous edition of this book has been cataloged by the Library of Congress.
ISBN: 978-0-8173-1886-4 (cloth)
E-ISBN: 978-0-8173-8895-9

Contents

FEATHERSTON PLACE
• HOLLY SPRINGS

LOCHINVAR
POPE •   • PONTOTOC
OLD MATHIS
PLANTATION

ERROLTON
COLUMBUS •
CASTALIAN   WAVERLEY
SPRINGS
DURANT •

WM. LAKE HOME
VICKSBURG
ANCHUCA

BEAUREGARD
• WESSON

NATCHEZ   • ELLISVILLE
DUNLEITH   AMOS DEASON HOME

COLD SPRING PLANTATION
• PINCKNEYVILLE

vii

Lochinvar is near Pontotoc.

The Faithful Caretaker
At Pontotoc

The hunt had been disappointing. Though the dogs had treed once, heralding their accomplishment to the country-side, the coon had escaped. So around midnight, after a cold rain had begun to fall, the hunters left the woods and took a short cut across a pasture to the road where they had parked their pick-up.

They were about halfway across the open pasture when they first saw the lantern bobbing toward them. At first they thought one of their companions had got separated from them in the dark and was trying to catch up. They stopped walking and called, "Yoo-hoo! Yoo-hoo! Come on! We're waiting! Come on!"

But though they shouted several times, there was no answer. The light kept moving closer, but its carrier was strangely silent.

Suddenly the men were uneasy, filled with foreboding.

"Hey," one of the group whispered (he later was not sure why he had whispered instead of speaking right out). "Hey—That's not one of us. We're all here—nobody's missing. Let's get out of here!"

They ran through the dark to their waiting pick-up, tumbled in, and sped toward Pontotoc.

Once they had reached the safety of the town, their fears subsided, but even the brightly-lighted streets and the familiar buildings did not entirely erase their feelings of uneasiness, of strangeness.

"What was it we saw?" they asked each other. "What kind of lantern was it?" And none of them had a satisfactory answer.

"It wasn't fox fire—not a jack-o-lantern—I've seen that glowing in the woods plenty of times. It wasn't that. I know it wasn't fox fire," one of the men asserted.

"It was a lantern for sure. But it wasn't right somehow. Something wasn't natural...."

"The way it moved was scary. Made me think it was threatening me in some way," his companion interrupted. "Sounds stupid to say I was afraid of a lantern—but I was."

Next morning when the hunters met for coffee at a Pontotoc cafe, their experiences of the night before still filled their thoughts and conversation. They re-told the events, much to the amusement of other coffee-drinkers who chided them with questions about what they had been drinking and teased them about their fears.

While the teasing was going on, an elderly man rose from his table at the rear of the cafe (after fifty years of regular patronage, he had become as familiar a part of the decor as the chrome napkin holders or the heavy sugar bowls with their hinged tops) and interrupted the chatter to ask,

"Where were you when you saw the light? Out near Lochinvar?"

"Why yes. We were taking a short cut across the pasture there. But how did you guess?"

"It wasn't a guess," the old man replied. "I've been listening to you all talk, and I was pretty sure you'd seen the

10

They ran through the dark to their waiting pick-up.

Lochinvar light. I've seen it, too. More than once. But it has been a long time since I've heard anybody talk about seeing it. I figured the light had gone away, vanished for good. I'm sort of glad to know that old Uncle Eb is still on the job at Lochinvar," he chuckled.

"Uncle Eb? Who's he?"

"He—his ghost, that is—was carrying that lantern you saw. Ebenezer Gordon, old and trusted slave of Colonel James Gordon. Still protecting that fine place just like his master told him to."

For a moment nobody spoke. The men looked at each other, stared at the old man, then looked away. Then one of them asked,

"You mean to say we saw a ghost—a real ghost—last night? Man, that's hard to believe!" He turned to his friends for reassurance.

Reassurance did not come though, at least not from the man seated beside him. That man looked straight at him and said slowly, "I believe it. I purely believe we saw a ghost, Uncle Eb with his lantern."

Uncle Eb's story is so closely entwined with Lochinvar it is almost impossible to separate the two.

Lochinvar is the home built by Robert Gordon, the Scotch adventurer, in the late 1830s as a gift for his wife, the former Miss Walton of Cotton Gin Port. The two had been married in a triple wedding ceremony which saw Mr. Walton give three of his daughters in marriage.

"Where do you want your house?" he would ask her. "Where would you like to live?" And he would describe for her possible home sites on the thousands of acres of land he owned in northern Mississippi. A shrewd speculator, handling money in a way that would have brought pride to his Scottish ancestors, Gordon at one time owned a strip of land stretching all the way from Pontotoc to Aberdeen, sixty miles away.

Aberdeen was Gordon's own town. He founded a trading post there in the early 1830s and named the place Dundee in honor of the town he loved in Scotland. But the way the natives pronounced the name, giving it such a slurring drawl that no true Scotsman would recognize it, irritated Gordon. He changed the town's name to Aberdeen.

Before Gordon had trained the settlers to give Aberdeen the proper Scottish accent, he moved northward to Pontotoc where the government land office had been established. The Chickasaw Indians had ceded their lands, and speculators were congregating in the area.

It was near Pontotoc that Gordon found the site for the house he planned to build. The location he chose was the home of a Choctaw chieftain, Chinubi. As soon as he saw the wooded ridge, Gordon knew it was the perfect place for his grand house, and he determined to get ownership of the land. So not long afterwards the aged Chinubi was removed, and Robert Gordon began building Lochinvar.

Slaves from the Gordon plantation felled giant pines and hewed them into sills, joists, beams, and boards. Artisans fitted the timbers into place, following sketches provided by Robert Gordon.

The four tall Doric columns to support the portico were shipped from Scotland (some Pontotoc residents said they came from a real castle) to Mobile and were brought overland by ox carts to Pontotoc. Spectators from all over the countryside came to watch those massive columns raised into place.

When the house was finished, Mr. and Mrs. Gordon invited their friends to come to a party, a social christening for Lochinvar. That party with its music and lights and feasting and dancing and laughter was one of James Gordon's earliest memories.

The little boy, only child of Robert and Mary Elizabeth, was dressed in a velvet suit with a ruffled shirt, and he was allowed to stand beside his parents as they greeted the guests. His parents introduced James proudly, and the lad behaved with charm and courtesy befitting the future master of Lochinvar.

It was Ebenezer, James' personal servant, who prepared James for the night, Ebenezer who saw that James' suit fit perfectly, that his long curls were smoothly brushed, that he remembered to shake hands with the men and to bow to the ladies. And it was Ebenezer who, hours later, carried a sleepy little boy upstairs to bed.

Looking back, James Gordon could not remember when Ebenezer had not been a part of his life. Ebenezer taught him to hunt and to fish, told him stories about "de critters," supervised his manners, and, when he was old enough, packed his trunks and watched him leave for the University of Mississippi at Oxford. That was in 1851.

It was hard to tell exactly when Ebenezer became old, but sometime during those years when James was growing up, Ebenezer slipped past the invisible but inflexible time line that marks the arrival of old age. Having reached that milepost, he became known as Uncle Eb. Though he knew the title signified affection and respect, Ebenezer winced the first few times he heard himself called Uncle, and he found it particularly upsetting to have James Gordon, his young master, call him Uncle Eb.

James, home from college, felt uncomfortable about using the title. He embraced his friend and said honestly, "You don't look a bit older than you did when I was a little boy."

"Black wears well," Ebenezer—Uncle Eb—replied. He, too, wondered where the years had gone.

As time passed, they both became accustomed to the

title, just as they adapted to other changes the years brought.

In February, 1856, James married Miss Virginia Wiley whom he had known while he was a student at Oxford. In December their daughter, Annie, was born.

From the time she began to walk, Annie adored Uncle Eb. She delighted in slipping away from the maid her mother chose for her and following after Uncle Eb. She begged him to sing to her or to tell her a story or to push her in the swing. Delighted, he obliged.

"You just like yo' papa," he would say proudly.

"No," Annie would correct him. "Papa is a boy. I'm a girl!"

"You just like him though," Uncle Eb insisted.

Then came The War.

Robert Gordon, too old to become actively involved, gave his support and advice as James raised a company of Confederate cavalry, the first from northern Mississippi.

Before Captain James Gordon rode away to Richmond, he called Uncle Eb to him.

"Take care of my family and of the plantation," Captain Gordon said. "My father needs your help, and I need to know that you are protecting my wife and little Annie. Don't let anything happen to them. I'll be back before long."

He pulled the old black man into his arms, and if there were tears, only the two of them knew.

Thus began Uncle Eb's role as protector of the Gordon family and their property. Late every afternoon he would begin his rounds, checking to make sure the gates were closed and the doors to the big house were locked (they had never been locked before), that the fires were safely banked, and that no strangers were lurking about the place.

He moved a pallet to the wide upstairs hall, putting it just outside Annie's door. "I'm right here if you want me, Little Miss. Uncle Eb is right here," he assured her.

15

When the child, restless and disturbed by the changes in her life, would wake and whimper, "Uncle Eb, I hear something," he would answer, "Don't you fret, baby. Uncle Eb will go see. Just let me get my lantern."

Then Uncle Eb with his lantern would tiptoe down the stairs and walk out into the yard to satisfy the child—and himself—that nothing was wrong.

Just as he learned to pacify the child, he became competent at other unfamiliar skills. As the war dragged on, he learned to make repairs on the house and on the farm equipment. He learned to make do with plain fare instead of the sumptuous meals once served at Lochinvar. He learned to patch and mend and darn and do without.

Most importantly, perhaps, he learned to nurse the sick and wounded Confederate soldiers who, in greater and greater numbers, found their way to Lochinvar.

He slept fitfully, as many old people do, and he lay listening to the night sounds, cataloging each one. Sounds he could not identify, he crept outside to investigate. Holding his lantern high, he wandered about in the darkness until he assured himself that nothing was amiss.

Night after night after night the circle of light from Uncle Eb's lantern darted about the house, the barn, the garden, the pasture, the orchards as he reassured himself that the people and property entrusted to his care were secure.

Toward that circle of light Captain Gordon rode one night.

"Who's there?" Uncle Eb challenged.

"It's me—James!" came the reply. James Gordon swung down from his saddle. "I'm home!"

The officer's stay at Lochinvar was brief. A few days later James Gordon, risen to the rank of colonel, returned to combat with the Second Mississippi Cavalry Regiment, Armstrong's Brigade.

Colonel Gordon and Uncle Eb never met again.

One cold, rainy night Uncle Eb was roused from sleep by an unfamiliar sound. Lighting his lantern, he went out into the dark. He was soaked to the skin before he was convinced that everything was all right. A day or two later, what had seemed to be a mild cold developed into pneumonia. There was no doctor to summon, no medicine to give. In less than a week Uncle Eb was dead.

It was a long time before Colonel Gordon received the news of Uncle Eb's death. He was in England at the time on a mission for Confederate President Jefferson Davis to arrange the purchase of a privateer, a trim ship that could slip through the Yankee blockades.

On his way home, as soon as he landed in North Carolina, he was captured and imprisoned aboard ship at Old Point Comfort. Escaping, he made his way to Canada. In Canada he met an entertaining man named John Wilkes Booth. This casual acquaintanceship with Booth later pointed suspicion to the Mississippi officer when President Abraham Lincoln was assassinated, but Colonel Gordon was able to prove his innocence.

These events delayed Colonel Gordon's receipt of the letter which told him, "Uncle Eb is dead. He was faithful to the last, going out into the rain with his lantern to make sure that no enemy had come to Lochinvar to harm us."

Since the old man's death came before the war ended, before his beloved Master James returned to Lochinvar, Uncle Eb never knew that he had been relieved of his responsibility, that it was no longer necessary for him to roam protectively about Lochinvar's acres with his lantern.

So Uncle Eb—or his ghost—continues his faithful vigil.

Cold Spring plantation near Pinckneyville.

"I'll Wait Forever!"

"Edna," stormed Mr. Reed, "go break that window! I'm tired of having people—strangers!—come out here to Cold Spring asking to see the face in the window. Makes me feel like we're operating some sort of freak show.

"It's gotten to where we don't have any privacy with curiosity-seekers coming all the time. Just break that window and be done with it!"

So Mrs. Reed, dutiful wife, went upstairs and smashed the window pane, destroying forever the likeness of the young woman etched upon it.

Nobody is quite sure what the young woman's first name was, though it is generally accepted that her last name was McGehee. It would almost have to be: McGehees have lived at Cold Spring for more than a century and a quarter, seven generations of them.

Perhaps, they say, she was the daughter of Edward McGehee who, with his wife (the former Miss Anna B. Carter) moved to Cold Spring plantation in February, 1845.

Shortly before The War, about 1859 or 1860, the story goes, Miss McGehee (some storytellers insist her name was

Catherine) fell foolishly and happily and completely in love with a young man whom she met at a holiday party at her grandfather's home, Bowling Green, near Woodville.

Catherine, if indeed that was her name, had ridden with other members of her family in a caravan of buggies and wagons (trunks and servants rode in the wagons) from Cold Spring to Bowling Green to spend the Christmas season.

Though the day of the journey was sunny and mild for December, Catherine welcomed the warmth from the heated bricks her maid had wrapped in flannel and placed beneath her feet. There had been no rain for more than a week, so the road from Pinckneyville to Woodville was in unusually good condition and there was no danger of having a vehicle mire down axle-deep in red mud or slip off the narrow roadbed into a gully. The trip was gratefully uneventful with brief stops at the homes of friends along the way to break the monotony.

Catherine was not bored. When she tired of listening to the conversations in the buggy, she let her mind wander to Bowling Green and to the preparations for the party being made there. When she closed her eyes—she nodded off a time or two—she could see the smilax laced through the spindles of the long stairway, the boughs of holly, the tall Christmas tree with its star brushing the frescoed ceiling, the logs burning in the wide fireplaces in the double parlors, the musicians tuning their fiddles in the back hall, the silver punch bowls filled with eggnog, and the candles—hundreds and hundreds of candles everywhere.

After she had, in her imagination, set the scene for the party, Catherine asked herself, "Who will be there? Who will ask me to dance?" She dozed off to sleep as the horses' hoofs echoed her questions: "Who will be there? Who will ask me to dance? Who will be there? Who will ask me to dance? Who will..."

The man who asked her to dance was John Howell (at least that is the name some people recall), newly arrived in Woodville. He requested the honor of being her partner again and again and again so that she had no dances left for her cousins or for the young gentlemen who had paid her court on previous visits.

John Howell was the most exciting partner Catherine had ever danced with, and as they swirled and pivoted about the floor, she wondered where he had learned to dance, where he had come from. But though she asked several rather direct questions, she found out very little about him.

He spoke vaguely of business associations with her grandfather, Judge Edward McGehee, and Catherine assumed that he had a position of prominence with her grandfather's railroad, The West Felician. Later she decided he was, perhaps, a cotton broker from New Orleans, and then it occurred to her that he might be a lawyer. By the time they went in to supper, she cared very little where he came from or what he did. All that mattered was that he was beside her.

Hours later, when the party was over and when the last guest had gone, Catherine paused a minute to choose a pink camellia from an arrangement on the hall table: she planned to press the flower as a memento of the night.

From the landing, a cousin called down teasingly, "Catherine's got a beau!" Other cousins hanging over the railing took up the chant, "Catherine's got a beau! Catherine's got a beau!"

Catherine's blush was almost as bright as the camellia she held.

From that night until her visit ended, John Howell was a frequent caller at Judge McGehee's home, escorting Catherine to dances, to supper parties, to church. He seemed to be as charmed by Catherine as she was by him. Two or three times when they were alone (privacy is rare in a household overflowing with holiday guests), he seemed about to talk seriously with her regarding their future together, but on each occasion he paused suddenly, then laughed and talked instead of some amusing happening he had witnessed.

He did, however, promise that he would come calling on Catherine at Cold Spring.

"You'll never find Cold Spring," Catherine told him.

"Oh, yes I will!" he replied. "I'll come riding out in style on your grandfather's railroad."

"You'll never get to Cold Spring by train," Catherine corrected him. "Grandfather didn't build his railroad to Pinckneyville. When I was a little girl, I used to beg him to build me a railroad out to my house, but he never did."

"Well," John said, "I'll come by boat then."

"You surely know that Pinckneyville is not on the river!" Catherine retorted. She was becoming tired of his game.

John sensed her irritation. "I'm sorry," he said. "I shouldn't tease about visiting you. I'll come. I promise I'll come. I'll build me a railroad or dig me a river to get there if I have to, but I'll come! Before the new year is many days old, I'll be at Cold Spring with you."

"I'll be waiting," Catherine promised.

And she did wait.

She did not expect John's arrival at Cold Spring until several days after her return home, of course, but when a week had elapsed, Catherine hurried out into the hall to peer through the sidelights by the heavy front door each time she heard horses approaching. And each time she tried to hide her disappointment when she recognized the riders as neighbors coming for a visit or as men coming to see her father on business.

As the days passed without John's arrival and without word from him, Catherine began spending more and more time alone in her upstairs bedroom. Except to join her family for meals, Catherine seldom came downstairs. Sometimes she read, and occasionally she did a bit of embroidery. She wrote a dozen or more letters to John, but she burned each one of them.

Most of the time Catherine sat at the window, leaning her forehead against the windowpane and gazing down the tree-shaded lane that led to the house.

Her parents became increasingly concerned about Catherine, and they tried to arrange outings and pleasures for her, but she pleaded headaches and other vague discomfitures so that she could remain at home.

Her father suggested that they all go to New Orleans for the Mardi Gras festivities, and he even promised Catherine a whole new wardrobe for the Carnival balls, but she showed no interest in the trip.

Mr. McGehee went on business to Woodville where he made inquiries about John Howell, inquiries which he berated himself for not having made earlier.

When he returned to Cold Spring, he called Catherine to him and told her, "Catherine, my dear, you must stop waiting for John Howell. I regret to have to say this to you, but he will never come. He...."

"It's not true!" Catherine interrupted. "He will come! He will! I will wait for him forever!" She ran up the stairs to her room and slammed the door.

Her mother started to go up to comfort her—Catherine's muffled sobbing enveloped the house like a pall—but Mr. McGehee stopped her. "No," he said. "Leave her alone. Facing the truth can break a heart, but she must face this truth."

Nobody at Cold Spring or at Pinckneyville knew for certain what "this truth" was. Mr. McGehee never shared fully with anyone, not even with his wife, the truth he had learned about John Howell.

There were rumors that old Judge McGehee had sent John Howell away, feeling that he was not acceptable as a suitor for Catherine. Some people said John Howell was a riverboat gambler who had posed as a relative of a socially prominent Wilkinson County family, and others said he was an unscrupulous slave trader. There was even a report that he was married with a wife and family (two children? three?) living in southwest Louisiana. No one ever knew for certain.

After the confrontation with her father, Catherine's appearances at meals became spasmodic, and she seldom touched the trays of food sent up to her room. Except for her daily Bible chapter, she never read anything, and her needle rusted in the linen embroidery square she had been stitching.

Hour after hour and day after day, she sat close to the window listening for hoofbeats and looking for a rider who never came.

Servants walking beneath the window grew accustomed to looking up and seeing Catherine there. "Po' little miss," they'd say, "grieving for that white trash."

One night during a severe storm, Catherine thought she heard John coming and she called his name, but it was only the thunder she heard and the wind-tossed branches beating a tattoo against the house. The vivid, almost-incessant flashes of lightning illuminated the landscape, and Catherine leaned close to the window, hoping to see John Howell riding toward the house. But she only saw swaying trees tethered by soggy tangles of moss, and rivulets of rain filling the ruts in the drive. She sat at the window until the storm had ended, and then she went to bed. She placed a faded camellia on her bedside table.

Catherine never left her bed again, never sat beside the window again. A few days later, after a strangely brief illness,

Catherine died.

There was some speculation that John Howell might come for the funeral, but he did not. After awhile most people forgot about him, and in later years, only the real romantics ever connected Catherine's death with a tragic love affair.

It was a day or two after her funeral that servants walking across the yard near Catherine's room glanced up at her window, as they had become accustomed to doing.

"Look!" one of them exclaimed. "It's Miss Catherine—she's still looking out the window!"

Surely enough, there etched on the pane was the distinct likeness of a young woman. She was looking, as she had for so long, across the yard toward the road.

Some people who saw the image said it was a natural phenomenon, that a flash of lightning had imprinted Catherine's likeness on the wet glass in the same way that a photographer takes a picture on film. It was all quite logical, though an extremely rare occurrence, they said.

But other people remembered hearing Catherine say, "I'll wait for him forever." For years, until the pane was broken, these people would gesture toward the window and say,

"There she is. Still waiting."

If the window is broken and the likeness of an eternally hopeful young woman is no longer visible, there is another ghost at Cold Spring, a ghostly legend about the builder of the house.

His name was Dr. John Carmichael, an Army surgeon, and he founded the plantation in the late 1790s.

When time came to build his home (the actual date of construction is not definite), Dr. Carmichael selected fine blue poplar timber, and he brought stonemasons to fit together the flagstones for the front and rear porches and to supervise the laying of the brick foundation for Cold Spring.

Around the front porch, linking the four tall columns, and around the arched entryway at the rear, Dr. Carmichael had iron fences erected. The front fencing looked like a plain wooden bannister with sharp pickets across the top while the ironwork at the rear of the house was taller and more ornate with brass decorations atop the posts.

The installation of the ironwork, Dr. Carmichael explained, was necessary to protect the occupants of the house from marauding wild animals.

Protection of another kind was provided by the Masonic emblem which Dr. Carmichael hung from the open archway over the back porch.

Dr. Carmichael was pleased with his house, and he showed off with pride the 18-inch wide blue poplar boards in the walls, the flagstone porches, the protective iron railings, the hand-carved Masonic emblem, and the fine furnishings. His greatest joy, however, was to show off his wine cellar.

The master of Cold Spring liked to drink. He collected fine wines and whiskeys as avidly as other men collected guns or horses, and he delighted in sharing his collection with guests who truly appreciated the bouquet, the color, the smoothness, and the flavor of the beverages. Sometimes— rather often, in fact—Dr. Carmichael would move his rocking

The master of Cold Spring liked to drink.

chair to a point where he could see his racks of wine and kegs of whiskey, and then he would rock in pleasant contentment as he savored a drink and admired his supply.

Before his death, Dr. Carmichael made rather unusual arrangements for his funeral. His instructions, plainly set forth in his will, were that he be laid to rest by his friends. These friends, he instructed, were to place his coffin near the wine cellar. Then they were to consume the contents of that cellar—every drop—before they buried him.

His friends dutifully carried out the doctor's wishes. They assembled at Cold Spring. They prepared the body for burial. They placed the coffin near the wine cellar. And they drank.

Next day (or was it the day after that?) when they began to sober up, the friends began trying to recall the details of the funeral. To their dismay, they discovered that a major detail—the location of Dr. Carmichael's grave—was missing from their memory. Nobody in the assemblage could remember where they had buried their old friend.

Just as they were about to organize a search party, one of their group stepped forward with the welcome announcement that he recalled where Dr. Carmichael had been laid to rest, and he led them unerringly to the fresh grave.

Some time later, Dr. Carmichael's body was exhumed and taken to Woodville for a more decorous burial. Even that journey was marked by mishaps. The coffin, so they say, fell from the wagon maybe half a dozen times, and two or three times its absence was not discovered until the empty wagon had traveled quite a distance. Then the route had to be retraced, the wayward coffin had to be found and reloaded on the wagon before the journey could continue.

Even though the burial in Woodville was eventually accomplished quite properly, there is evidence that the unconventional spirit of Dr. Carmichael never left Cold

Spring.

There are times, particularly in the late afternoons, when there is the unmistakable sound of a rocking chair swaying with contented squeaks near Dr. Carmichael's wine cellar.

When they hear the sound, the occupants of Cold Spring nod and say, "There's Dr. Carmichael, back to admire his wine cellar and ready to share a toddy with a convivial friend."

Tracks where trainmen saw the light in Beauregard.

Flag Stop

Sometimes when customers gather around the cluttered counter at Smith's One Stop in Beauregard, the talk turns to the mysterious light that plagued railroad crews there back in the 1920s.

Some folks still think, as some thought then, that the light was swamp gas—fox fire—the Illinois Central trainmen saw beside the tracks those many nights. But now, as then, other observers point out that the track area is high and dry, no suitable site for this phenomenon.

Others jokingly say the light was likely old Jack-O-Lantern himself hunting for a place to start his own Hell. And, for the benefit of those who don't know it, they tell the old folk tale about how Jack, one of the meanest men who ever breathed, died and went to Hell. Jack was so bad and so strong that the Devil was afraid of him, scared he would disrupt Hell. So the Devil gave Jack a chunk of fire and urged him to go start his own Hell. Jack with his chunk of fire is still roaming around looking for a proper site for Hell, the tale goes, and lots of times the strange lights people see are really just Jack-O-Lantern still hunting a place to settle.

Nobody believes that story, of course, though it was said that at one time Beauregard would have fitted the qualifications for Hell as well as any town in Mississippi. Better than any, maybe.

They used to tell about a drunk passenger who went to sleep in the day coach of a train chugging through southern Mississippi. The conductor came through the coach taking up tickets, and waked the snoring man to ask where he was going.

"I'm going to Hell," the passenger replied.

"All right. Go back to sleep. I'll put you off at Beauregard," the conductor said.

That was the kind of reputation the town had.

Such a reputation was not entirely undeserved. Beauregard had seven saloons lined up along the railroad tracks, saloons so big and so busy that visitors from cities such as Jackson, Vicksburg, or even New Orleans itself were amazed and impressed.

Those saloons flourished during the 1870s and early 1880s when the Mississippi Mills at nearby Wesson, less than two miles away, were prospering. Back then, the mill was the largest cotton manufacturing plant in the world, and it operated around the clock, twenty-four hours a day.

Furthermore, by 1880 Mississippi Mills had electric lights, a marvel that people traveled hundreds of miles to see. After they had seen the miracle of illuminated darkness, many of them stopped in Beauregard's saloons to refresh themselves and to discuss the amazing display of electrical energy they had seen.

On the days when the workers at Mississippi Mills got their wages, Beauregard's saloons were so crowded and the throngs of people there were so rowdy that prudent people stayed off the streets entirely.

Beauregard was the kind of place—though there were

lots of good people among its populace—that preachers were prone to compare with Sodom and Gomorrah, and many of them thundered the prediction that because of its wickedness, Beauregard would be destroyed.

It almost was.

One Sunday afternoon in April, 1883, a cyclone came whirling down on the town with such force that it sucked the brick curbing out of an 82-foot well and blew a two-by-four clean through the trunk of a big red oak tree.

That cyclone also destroyed the infamous saloons and flattened the Baptist Church. It swept away the old and the new Methodist churches, the hotel, the post office, little Mrs. Holloway's millinery shop (they say she created the loveliest hats in southern Mississippi), the livery stable, the town hall, the mayor's office, two schools, the academy, and thirty-five dwellings.

Only three houses in the town escaped heavy damage. One of those houses belonged to Jim Kelly (there were three Jim Kellys in Beauregard: Lying Jim, Butcher Jim, and Honest Jim—this was Honest Jim's house), and family members recall that he brought scores of injured persons to his home. After the rooms and the halls were filled with people, he laid them in rows on the wide gallery.

Another of the homes left unscathed was the residence of Dr. Elias Alford Rowan, who may have been one of the busiest men in Copiah County during the terrible days after the cyclone.

This home of Dr. Rowan's was big, three stories tall with twenty-three rooms and eleven porches. When he built it, only two years before the storm struck, Dr. Rowan had thought he might use it as a hospital, but that plan did not materialize.

Then for a few April days his rambling house fulfilled the mission he had once envisioned for it.

33

He was a remarkable man, this Dr. Rowan.

For one thing, in a town famous for its saloons and for its drinking bouts, Dr. Rowan was an outspoken prohibitionist. Perhaps it was his professional observations of the effects of excessive drinking or perhaps it was his firm Baptist doctrine which prompted his support of prohibition. Whatever it was that motivated him, Dr. Rowan became a leader in the anti-liquor movement in his state.

The doctor was so admired and respected in his home town that despite what would appear to be a very unpopular stand on the liquor question, he was elected to the Mississippi Legislature. It was in large measure due to his efforts that Mississippi became a dry state.

Then there was the matter of his pigeon cote. Not many people around Beauregard cared enough about pigeons to provide fancy living quarters for the birds. Dr. Rowan did.

The house he built for his pigeons rivaled his own massive home, though on a smaller scale, of course. The cote was octagonal and several stories high with perches and galleries and other decorative touches. That pigeon house survived long after the Rowan house was torn away.

Dr. Rowan was remarkable for his church work, too. For fifteen years, the Sunday School at the Wesson Baptist Church, where he served as superintendent, was the largest in the state with an enrollment of more than 400.

And though it may seem unlikely, Dr. Rowan could be most remarkable for his role in the drama of the mysterious lights along the railroad right-of-way in Beauregard.

That story began in 1926.

An engineer on the Illinois Central was guiding his train through Beauregard one night, going at a good clip, when he saw a lantern swinging back and forth down the track.

"What's that?" he asked his brakeman, who was in the cab with him.

"Looks like somebody is trying to flag us down," the brakeman answered. "We'd better stop."

So the engineer began slowing the engine down, keeping his eyes on the swinging lantern all the time. He stopped the train right where the light had signaled, but when he and the brakeman looked out, no one was there.

"What do you want?" the engineer shouted. He felt a little foolish shouting into the darkness. There was no reply.

He and the brakeman got out of the engine and walked along the tracks for some distance, but they neither saw nor heard anyone.

All the way to McComb they wondered who—or what—had been flagging the train.

The engineer, as soon as he got to McComb, reported the incident to the district superintendent. After he had finished telling about the swinging lantern that vanished, the superintendent said teasingly,

"Happened at Beauregard, did it? I thought that old saloon town had dried up. Sure you and your buddy didn't stop there and get a drink or two?" The railroad official didn't take the report seriously, not at all.

His skeptical attitude tempted the engineer not to make a report when the same thing happened a few nights later, but he did.

"I know you won't believe this," he told the superintendent, "but that same light flagged us down at Beauregard last night. When I stopped the train and we got out to investigate, nobody was there.

"That lantern was waving until we stopped—we were looking straight at it—and then it disappeared instantly. You may not believe it, but it happened."

The superintendent did not believe it—what sensible man believes in ghostly lanterns?—and again he teasingly warned the engineer about drinking on the job.

"That lantern was waving until we stopped."

A few days later, however, when the crew of another Illinois Central train told of having been flagged down by a phantom lantern at Beauregard, the railroad official listened intently, and he did no teasing.

At the fourth report of the swinging lantern, the superintendent took notes and filed them in a pigeonhole in his rolltop desk.

The reports continued. So many train crews told of being stopped by a swinging lantern, a disappearing lantern, at Beauregard that the superintendent felt compelled to make a report to his superiors in the organization. He was afraid that they would laugh at him, just as he had scoffed at the first stories of the strange lantern, but they did not.

In fact, the higher-ups took his report so seriously that they sent railroad detectives to investigate. The detectives interviewed everyone who had seen the light, and they carefully wrote down the accounts the men gave of their experiences. The stories were all similar, and they were all in accord on the major details.

When the detectives compiled their findings, they realized that the light always reportedly appeared at the same location: all the crews saw the light near Dr. Rowan's old home on the edge of town. The investigators began asking questions about the place.

They learned that the house had been vacant for some time but that it remained completely furnished, even to the medical instruments and the classical library of its builder.

The house looked haunted. No repairs had been made for years, and its broken windows stared out through a tangle of vines and weeds. Already ghostly legends were growing about the Rowan place, and venturesome boys dared each other to spend the night there.

Those tales of ghosts were prompted by the sudden deaths of four persons closely connected with the Rowan family, the detectives were told, and with each passing year more and more people reported seeing "strange things" at the dilapidated house and of hearing eerie noises there.

Gradually the furnishings in the house disappeared. Medical texts, theological treatises and leather-bound books of poetry were scattered beneath the cedar trees and into the woods beyond. By the early 1940s, only the decaying shell of the house remained. The fine millwork was sold to a builder in Brookhaven, and what remained of the Rowan Place was demolished.

All that came later though, after the long investigation of the disappearing lantern.

One day, after they had poked around the deserted Rowan house, the detectives asked a neighbor, "What became of Dr. Rowan? What happened to him?"

"He got killed," the neighbor answered. "It was about 1912, I believe. Anyhow, Dr. Rowan was getting old, up in his seventies, when he got killed."

"Who killed him?"

"One of your trains did, ran over him and killed him right here in Beauregard. As I remember, Dr. Rowan had gone down to the train to meet a patient of his who was coming here for treatment. Some people say Dr. Rowan had been to Jackson on business and had come back on the train, the same train that killed him. I believe though that he had gone to meet a patient who came from up the line.

"Anyhow, he was walking down the track—there was a double track, you know—with his back to the engine. The engineer blew at him, but Dr. Rowan sort of got confused—like I said, he was up in his seventies—and instead of stepping out of the way, he stepped right in front of the engine.

"He screamed, 'Stop!' but the train couldn't stop.

"Yessir, the train ran over him and killed him right here in Beauregard."

The detectives listened with interest and recorded the information in their pocket-size notebooks. They were about to walk away when the man said,

"Listen. You don't suppose that's Dr. Rowan's ghost swinging that lantern and flagging down those trains, do you?

"Might be he's still troubled over losing his life so sudden like, and maybe he's still trying to stop the train. Maybe that's why he's waving that lantern. It might be him. Or his ghost."

It might have been.

The phantom lantern continued to flag down trains for two or three years, and though detectives continued to conduct thorough investigations, they were never able to find the source of the light. They could never explain its sudden appearances and disappearances. Nor could anyone else.

Dr. Elias Alford Rowan was a remarkable man.

A section of the original Natchez Trace.

Where The Witches Danced

South of Tupelo, after the Natchez Trace has wound past an old Chickasaw Indian village and past the Monroe Mission where churchmen proposed to civilize the Choctaws and past the site where the U. S. land agents set up headquarters back in 1801, a sign beside the Trace proclaims:

WITCH DANCE

Some motorists, their curiosity aroused, pull over into the parking area to read the rest of the sign:

The old folks say the witches once gathered
here to dance, and that wherever their feet touched
the ground the grass withered and died, never to
grow again.

Most of the people who read the sign laugh about the foolishness of putting up such a marker, and they drive away to wherever they were going.

A few people, more inquisitive and less hurried, go in search of the scorched spots where the witches danced, and some of them, the persistent ones, find the strange bare patches of earth in the thick grass. These rings of hard, baked earth look as if they have been there on the Trace for a long,

long time.

And, though they do not believe in witches, sometimes the people who find the scattered spots wonder about their origin and wonder who else has paused along the Trace to stare and speculate.

WITCH DANCE

Witch Dance -- the very name conjures visions of eerie midnights, swirling black capes, and brooms stacked against a nearby tree! The old folks say the witches once gathered here to dance, and that wherever their feet touched the ground the grass withered and died, never to grow again.

Impossible?-- maybe so, but look around, look for a hidden spot where no grass grows.

UNITED STATES DEPARTMENT OF THE INTERIOR
NATIONAL PARK SERVICE

Did De Soto see those small, parched clearings when he crossed the Trace in 1541? Or was the Spanish explorer so absorbed in his search for riches that he failed to notice the circles of bare earth?

The Indians, the Chickasaws and the Choctaws, who had followed this trail through the wilderness for five hundred years or more before De Soto's arrival surely knew about the witches' dances and the scars they left on the earth. Indian ponies, they say, shied around the sites where legend says the witches danced, and even the bravest warriors carefully avoided letting their moccasins touch a place where a witch's foot had been.

Lorenzo Dow, his gaunt frame swathed in a flapping coat, may have seen the bare spots along the Trace as he rode, head bowed in thought, to preach the Gospel in the river settlements. And if Lorenzo Dow did see the spots and if he knew of their significance, he likely preached about them in one of his wild hellfire-and-damnation sermons.

Andrew Jackson, he of the red hair and fiery temper, returning to Tennessee with Rachel, his bride, likely knew the story of the witches' dances, and he and Rachel may have reined in their horses and dismounted to examine closely the marks left on the land by the evil dancers.

Settlers, moving with their skimpy household goods and their big families to new homes in the Mississippi Territory, may have seen the witches' marks when they camped along the Trace. Those settlers, however, had no time to indulge in superstitious worry about the possible presence of evil spirits; their concern was with the real and constant threat of attack by hostile Indians or ruthless outlaws.

Burly, rowdy boatmen, bound overland for Tennessee or Kentucky after poling their flatboats down the Mississippi River to New Orleans, cared little for tales of witches. Like the settlers whom they met along the narrow wilderness road, their only thought was to avoid being robbed or murdered— or both—on the Trace.

All travelers on the Trace shared that same fear, a smothering awareness that Death claimed the Trace as his bailiwick, and that, as trespassers, they courted Death's fury. Though they banded together for their journeys along the narrow pathway (how many buffalo, how many deer had beat out the path with their hoofs?), their puny efforts to ward off danger were too often futile.

"It's not the physical hardships I dread—not being hungry or being wet and cold from crossing streams or being chewed on by swarms of insects—it is having fear as a constant companion," one traveler explained.

"You look up and you see buzzards circling over the Trace, and you know somebody has been murdered and left to rot. And you wonder—though you try not to—when the buzzards will come for you."

Witches? Who could bother about them under such circumstances?

One man who frequented the Trace did bother about witches. His name was Joseph Thompson Hare, and he came to the Trace to refine the art of robbery and of murder as practiced by his brutal, bestial predecessors, Big Harpe and Little Harpe.

Those earlier outlaws, Big Harpe and his younger brother, were certainly not the kinds of men who would have been awed or frightened by the footprints of witches. In fact, the appearances of the witches themselves would not have upset the bloodthirsty pair: they would have welcomed an eye-gouging, broomstick-swinging fight with them.

There is a story, told by what is generally referred to as a reliable source, that on one occasion when an Indian guide pointed out the witches' dancing spot to Big Harpe and told him the legend, Big Harpe deliberately stepped in the middle of each bare spot he could find. And as he hopped about, improvising a sort of dance of his own, he shouted uncouth challenges to any witches who might be listening.

Big Harpe had no answer from the witches that day, but

a few years later the ruffian fell victim to such fiendish treatment that it seemed the witches might have answered his challenge, might have been involved in his gory death.

It was like this:

After the Harpes had committed bloody atrocities on the Trace for several years, they retreated to Kentucky where they continued to torture, mutilate, rob, and murder. Following a particularly vicious murder (Big Harpe stabbed a woman and her baby to death and then set fire to their cabin to destroy their bodies), a posse captured Big Harpe. The husband of the murdered woman cut off Harpe's head with the outlaw's own knife (Harpe was alive and conscious during the slow decapitation) and mounted that hideous trophy on a tree beside the road.

Later, after the sun and rains had bleached it well, an old hill woman who had the reputation of being a conjure woman and a witch, took Big Harpe's skull out of the tree and ground it into a powder. She added the powder to other concoctions and dosed her nephew with the mixture to cure his fits.

Back in Mississippi, along the Trace where the witches danced, travelers told the tale of Big Harpe's death and of his powdered skull converted into a potion by a witch. And some people said, when the story was told, that there was a sound like cackling laughter along the Trace. It could have been the tall canes crackling, of course, but they said it sounded like witches chortling.

Among the people who heard the story of Harpe's head was Joseph Thompson Hare. The account intrigued yet disturbed him.

Hare himself would never have taunted the witches. Spirits troubled him, tormented him, during the years he roamed the Trace, and of all the passers-by who saw the witches' imprints, Hare would have been most likely to seek an explanation, a serious explanation, in the realm of the supernatural.

Unlike the Harpes, Hare was literate. He not only could read, he did. It was a skill that brought him little pleasure: the material he read seemed invariably to underline his miserable forebodings about the fate toward which he plunged.

Hare was something of a dandy. As a boy growing up in Philadelphia, he was apprenticed to a tailor for two years. Though he did not care for cutting patterns or for sewing seams, Hare did acquire a taste for fine fabrics and well-cut garments.

An old hill woman who had the reputation of being a conjure woman and a witch took Big Harpe's skull out of the tree and ground it into a powder.

Even then he could pick a pocket as quickly as he could snip a basting thread. He recognized that his talents at thievery were being wasted, so he left the tailor shop and signed aboard a sailing vessel. A month later, when the ship docked at New Orleans, Hare went ashore and never returned to sea.

Hare found New Orleans exciting—and expensive. He needed money, more money than his smalltime trickery and thefts in New Orleans could provide.

So Hare took to the Trace.

There amid the canebrake, swamps, and desolation, Hare and three companions began preying on travelers. They had an auspicious beginning, taking between $12,000 and $13,000 (all in gold) from their first victims.

Hare replaced his fine clothes with rough garments, and he smeared his face with berry juices during the months he prowled along the Trace. He and his cohorts established a hideout in the deep cleft of a rock up in Chickasaw country where they had as their scout an old Indian brave known as Hayfoot.

It may have been Hayfoot who showed Hare the splotches of scorched earth and told him the legend of the witches' dance. Hare did not step in the witches' tracks nor did he shout discourteous messages to them.

He did become more and more moody, lying awake nights to wrestle with an awful sense of foreboding. The silences of the wilderness depressed him, filled him with a homesickness for the bustling, exciting noises of the city. The periphery sounds, the calls of birds and the cries of animals and the snapping of the canes, that intruded into that silence tormented him.

Moralists say it could have been his conscience that troubled Hare, but this is unlikely. Robbery and murder (he did not delight in senseless killing as the Harpes did, but he did not refrain from murder when he deemed it necessary) became easier and easier for the gifted Hare.

When he could bear the barren life on the Trace no longer, Hare and his friends went to Nashville to spend their loot (Hare, the gentleman, purchased in addition to a wardrobe of new clothes a gig, two horses, and a black boy to drive), going from there to Louisville, then back down the river to Natchez and New Orleans.

Their money gone, the outlaws returned to the Trace to replenish their funds. This time they set up headquarters in a cave closer to Natchez. Hare hoped to escape the moodiness which had plagued him earlier.

But the silences closed in on him again. This time the quiet was broken by the bellowing of alligators.

"Ugly creatures! Why do you cry?" Hare stormed. Their cries sounded like the wailing of children. Hare had heard many children cry, too many.

This time a visit to Pensacola provided the release Hare required. Once again he played the gentleman. He and his friends entertained at a fancy ball (he wrote in his journal that it cost them $300) to which the entire Spanish garrison town was invited.

Hare's hospitality was profitable: when he and his confederates were arrested on suspicion of being American spies, men who had been guests at the ball came to their aid and persuaded the authorities to free them.

Once more they returned to the Trace. As they rode northward, Hare read aloud articles written by John Wesley, the pious founder of Methodism. He, Hare, fell under the spell of the religious articles and pled with his henchmen to renounce their evil ways and turn to leading lives of righteousness. They were not moved by his preaching. Nor was he.

By the time they reached northern Mississippi, passing

again the area where the witches danced, they had taken more than $10,000 from victims they chanced upon on the Trace. The highwaymen divided the loot and separated, never to meet again.

Hare, greedy and grasping, was not satisfied with the amount of his hoard, so he stopped a drover and, after threatening to kill the man, took from him two pistols and a small amount of money.

Stuffing his booty inside his jacket, Hare galloped away. It was a clear, starlit night, ideal for tracking, and Hare feared the drover might bring a posse in pursuit of him, so he rode rapidly to escape capture.

Suddenly at the edge of the Trace, Hare saw a beautiful white horse. There was no rider, just the pale horse standing there and staring at Hare. The animal was large and perfectly formed, the kind of steed any gentleman would be proud to ride.

Hare slowed his own mount and approached the white horse cautiously. He was less than six feet away when the animal disappeared, vanished completely. There was not a sound.

Hare was shaken. He tried to explain the appearance and the disappearance of the white horse, but he could not. He struggled to fathom the meaning of the experience, but he could not. The symbolism frightened him.

Fearful and confused, Hare stopped at a nearby house to spend the night: he could not endure the silences of the Trace alone.

During the night, a posse came and captured Hare. He spent the next five years in jail, pondering the meaning of the appearance of the ghostly horse, writing his confessions, and reading his Bible.

The experience did not reform him. A year later (1818), Hare arranged and took part in a robbery of a mail coach near Harve-de-Grace, Maryland, far from the haunted Trace.

That robbery was carried out at night, and everything went well, providing the outlaws with $16,900 in money and goods.

It was during this robbery that Hare made a kind-hearted gesture which cost him his life. One of the victims

Suddenly at the edge of the Trace, Hare saw a beautiful white horse.

begged to have his watch returned to him. It was a family heirloom, he said. Hare was moved by the man's family pride, and he agreed to return the timepiece. Hare held a lantern high so that the light would fall on the pile of stolen jewelry and he could select the watch the man prized so highly. The lantern illumined the watch—and Hare's face.

Two days later when Hare was in a fine tailoring shop in Baltimore trying to decide between a crimson silk coat and a bold plaid jacket, the owner of the watch appeared in the store, recognized Hare, and had him arrested.

Hare was hanged on September 10, 1818, before 1,500 spectators.

Until death came, he talked of a strange white horse he had seen on the Natchez Trace not far from where the witches danced.

The Amos Deason home on the outskirts of Ellisville.

Out Of Devil's Den

"If old General Forrest and General Lowry and their men and forty-four bloodhounds can't catch us, I don't reckon we got too much to worry about with Amos McLemore—Major McLemore, I believe the Rebs call him—after us," drawled Newt Knight.

"Just the same," he continued, looking hard at the circle of men squatting around him, "We'd best be careful. McLemore was raised in these parts, and he knows the swamps and creek bottoms pretty good. So keep a sharp watch. If you see McLemore and his posse or if you see anything suspicious, just give the signal. We'll know what to do."

Knight was conferring with some of his followers, leaders of the 120 or so renegades who were hiding out in the thickets and caves and bayous along the Leaf River, Tallahala Creek, and Tallahoma Creek in Jones County. It was late summer, 1863, and Knight had been a fugitive for more than a year.

He never considered himself a Confederate deserter, though other people called him that—and worse. All he did, Knight contended, was leave a fight he did not believe in and go back home. There was a difference, he said.

The tall, handsome countryman had never wanted to get involved in the War Between the States. He backed his fellow Jones Countians who instructed their delegate to oppose secession at the Secession Convention in Jackson. The vote in Jones County, where there were few slaves and fewer large landholders, was 376 to 24 against leaving the Union. And, later, Knight was as angry as his neighbors were when they learned that their delegate had ignored their wishes and had voted for secession.

Knight delighted in the carnival rowdiness when Jones County men gathered in front of the courthouse in Ellisville and hanged the delegate (his name was J. D. Powell) in effigy.

But when war actually came, Newt Knight answered the Confederacy's call for men. He explained to the young officer in charge of recruits that he did not favor fighting but that he would not mind helping take care of the sick and wounded. If some of his neighbors wondered when and why Newt had become so peace-loving, they never put the question to him: nobody who knew him ever deliberately got Newt riled up. They used to say Newt's cold, hard eyes could wither an opponent before a blow was ever struck.

Be that as it may, Newt Knight was assigned as an orderly in the Seventh Mississippi Battalion. He apparently served satisfactorily if not enthusiastically until the Confederate Congress passed what was known as the Twenty Negro Law. Under the provisions of this law, any man who owned as many as twenty slaves was excused from military service to return home and oversee the raising of crops.

This legislation did not set well with Newt Knight. It underscored what he had felt all along, that it was "a rich man's war and a poor man's fight." So, though he did not own the required twenty slaves (he did not own any), he went home, too.

Once he got back to his familiar Leaf River surroundings, Newt spread the word that he was serving as protector for his family, his kinfolks and such friends as needed him. The presence of Confederate raiding parties, either the authorized or the unauthorized variety, would no longer be tolerated, Knight said.

Knight was angered by the tales he heard about those Rebel militiamen who "requisitioned" horses, cattle, and provender from farm families, and it occurred to him that he had perhaps been aligned, however briefly and insignificantly, with the wrong side. He covenanted with himself that if he ever had a chance, he would join up with the Union Army.

Meantime, he aimed to use guerrilla tactics against any Confederate forces that ventured into his territory, roughly Jones and part of Jasper counties.

A goodly scattering of other Piney Woods natives shared Knight's views. More and more of them took unofficial leave from Confederate service and quietly came back home. Many of them joined what became known as Newt Knight's Company, and by late 1862 Captain Newton Knight reportedly had 125 men under his command.

These men pledged unwavering loyalty to Knight. They also took an oath of secrecy, swearing that they would never tell where the company's hideout (it was named Devil's Den) was located, and that they would never disclose the meanings of the signals sounded on their hunting horns.

For if it was disillusionment and bitterness that brought the men together, it was the blasts from their homemade horns that united them in action.

In the early days when his company was a-borning Newt Knight reasoned that comrades could best communicate with each other by using hunting horns. He worked out a system of signals which each man committed to memory. With these signals, news was passed from man to man that enemies were in the area or that a meeting was to be held at the hideout or that a member's family needed help at home or some other such message.

Every man in the company had his own horn, shaped and decorated to suit his notion, but nobody had a horn as fine as the one that hung from Captain Knight's shoulder. His horn was solid black, blacker even than his curly hair, and it glowed with the soft patina of frequent and reverent buffings.

Each horn had a slightly different sound, and trained listeners could nearly always identify the individual blowers. Everybody recognized the sound of Newt Knight's horn.

Newt blew that black horn as expressively as a musician playing a fine and delicate instrument. He purely made it talk. When he put his horn to his lips and blew a warning that Confederate cavalry were in the area, he almost made the horn describe the markings of the Rebels' horses, and when he announced the raiding of a Confederate supply train, his horn practically itemized the loot.

Nobody who heard Newt's horn ever forgot how it sounded.

Tales about Newt Knight and his horn spread throughout southern Mississippi, and the man became something of a folk hero. Newt liked that role.

Newt and his men were well known, too, at Confederate headquarters in the state. There his reputation was not that of fearless hero but of ruthless renegade. Although Newt's activities were more a nuisance than a menace to the Confederate cause, the man himself became such a symbol of lawless defiance that his capture became a major objective. It seemed that some Confederate officers had rather catch Newt Knight than to take U. S. Grant or W. T. Sherman into custody.

When the military search parties could not find Newt, they reportedly shot or hanged several suspected members of his company, sometimes carrying out the executions in the presence of wives and children of the victims.

As the horns carried the message of each new death, Newt's hatred grew more bitter.

When he learned that Captain Amos McLemore had been dispatched to capture him and break up his gang, Newt knew he had a dangerous adversary. Although he publicly scoffed at McLemore's chance of capturing him, Newt was worried.

Not only was McLemore an expert woodsman who was familiar with all of Jones County, he also possessed a daredevil courage that prodded him to swagger into strongholds of Knight sympathizers seeking information about the fugitive's hiding places. Repeated reports of McLemore's forays into his domain convinced Newt that the officer must be killed.

"Looks like it's him or me," Newt remarked to one of his companions. "Looks like we're going to have to kill him before he learns too much."

Newt carefully planned an ambush.

He knew that Captain McLemore and two other officers were quartered at the home of Mr. and Mrs. Amos Deason in Ellisville. He planned to wait along the route the men usually took and shoot Captain McLemore as he returned from a day of reconnoitering.

On the afternoon that Knight set up the ambush, McLemore took another route home.

Having his plan go awry angered Knight but it did not deter him. "We'll just have to ride into Ellisville and shoot McLemore at the Deason house," he decided.

Knight chose two friends to accompany him to Ellisville on this mission of death.

It was mid-September. The late summer heat, which sometimes lingers into October, had been dispelled by a chilly rain. Though the rain soaked their clothes and made their ride uncomfortable, Knight was grateful for it: there was less danger that rustling dry leaves would betray their presence on the Deasons' premises. Also, the rain would keep people indoors and off the streets, thus lessening the likelihood of witnesses to the crime.

The trio stopped on the edge of town to make final plans, and Knight suggested that they draw straws for the "honor" of shooting McLemore. Knight failed to draw the short straw, the one assigned to the killer, and this worried him. He wanted to be the man who pointed the gun at McLemore and pulled the trigger. Furthermore, the man who drew the short straw had never killed a man before, and he was nervous. Knight was not sure the proposed gunman had the guts to carry out the assignment.

So as they neared the Deason house, Knight whispered, "I will do the shooting myself. You wait for me." He dismounted and handed the reins to one of his companions. Then he walked cautiously toward the house.

A low fence surrounded the yard. Knight climbed over it rather than run the risk of having the latch on the gate click or the hinges squeak. Staying in the shadows of the trees, Knight crept up to a window and peeped in.

He saw three Confederate officers sitting around an open fire. They obviously had been soaked by the September rain, just as Knight was, and they had spread their boots, coats, and hats out on the hearth to dry.

It had been some time since Knight had seen McLemore, and at first he was not sure which of the trio he was. Then McLemore laughed and tossed his head in an arrogant way he had, and Knight recognized the characteristic gesture.

Once he had positively identified his victim, Knight eased around to get him in his gun sight. McLemore offered an awkward target. From his position in the yard, Knight could not shoot McLemore without also having the bullet strike a stranger, a man whom he did not know and had no known reason to kill.

So Knight moved slowly toward the front of the house, reached up and pulled himself over the bannister and onto the porch. Stealthily he tiptoed to the door and tried the knob. The knob turned easily, and when Knight gently pushed the door, it opened. He slipped into the dark hall and sidled down the wall, feeling his way, until he reached the doorway of the room where the three officers were sitting.

While he cocked his gun with his right hand, Knight turned the door knob with his left hand, flung open the door, and fired point-blank at McLemore.

"Help me!" McLemore cried. He was dead before his body slumped to the floor.

Even before the futile plea for help was uttered, Knight fled from the house, bounded over the bannisters, and sprang astride his waiting horse. He disappeared in the rainy darkness.

McLemore's companions jumped from their chairs and ran barefooted after the fleeing assassin, but by the time they reached the edge of the yard, only the sounds of hoofbeats indicated the direction the gunman had taken.

The officers returned to the house to find McLemore's lifeless body lying in a creeping pool of blood. As soon as the body was moved, servants were called to clean the blood from the pine floor. The stains would not come out. The servants scrubbed first with cold water, bringing bucket after bucket of it from the well, and stiff palmetto brooms. The stain remained, red and ugly. Then they tried using strong lye soap on the spot, and then sand, and then a combination of both. The patterned stain was still quite distinct.

The servants became frightened and muttered something about "innocent blood calling for revenge," and they stopped scrubbing and left the house.

Rather than cause further disruption in their household, the Deasons let the servants go. They covered the spot with a small braided rug.

Several days later, efforts were renewed to remove the stain. Large pieces of sandstone were brought from the creek and were used to scrub the wide boards. The stain seemed to disappear, but in damp, rainy weather, like the night when Captain McLemore was murdered, it would seep through the wood again, as plain as ever.

Through the years, repeated efforts to scour away the

reminder of Captain McLemore's bloody death wore the floor thin. And always the stains came back.

Those stains may still be on the floor: a good many years ago the pine boards were covered with hardwood flooring. The present owners of the house, Mr. and Mrs. Welton Smith (she is a direct descendant of Amos and Ellen Deason), are tempted sometimes to tear the new flooring out and see if the stains are still there.

Though they are not certain about the existence of the stubborn blood stains, they do know that on certain dreary nights the knob on the door of the death room slowly turns and the door flies open. Nobody is ever there.

"It's Newt Knight," they say "old Newt coming back to the scene of his crime."

Newt Knight lived a long time after the War, lived to be an old man of 92. His final years were marked by turmoil and controversy just as his earlier years had been.

And a strange thing happened a few years before he died.

Newt knew he did not have long to live, and he wanted to make plans for his funeral. So one day he walked across the field and picked out the spot for his grave.

"I want to be buried here, right in the shade of this cedar tree," he said. He reached in his pocket, got his knife, and trimmed a few small, low limbs off the cedar tree as he talked.

It was not long before that healthy tree withered and died.

Folks who saw the dead cedar wondered, just as they wonder about the bloodstains on the floor at the Deason house and about the door that springs open when nobody is there.

And they tell again the legend of Newt Knight, the phantom who still comes out of Devil's Den.

Dunleith in Natchez.

The Long, Long Visit

"How long is she going to stay?" Sarah whispered to her mother.

Mrs. Dahlgren gave her young daughter a reproving look. Then on the pretext of going out of the parlor to inquire about the progress of supper, she motioned Sarah to follow her.

Out in the hall, out of earshot of the guest, Mrs. Dahlgren said softly but firmly, "Miss Percy will stay here at Dunleith as long as she likes. She is your kinswoman, Sarah, your cousin, and I expect you to show her every consideration and courtesy, both as kinswoman and as guest."

"But why did...?" Sarah started to ask.

Mrs. Dahlgren cut her short. "That is all," she said. "There will be no more questions about Miss Percy. None. Do you understand?"

Two of Sarah's younger brothers, rowdy and outspoken like their father, raced through the parlor and out into the hall.

"She talks funny," giggled one boy.

"She smells funny," added his brother.

Before their mother could rebuke them, they had run from the hall out onto the porch where they tussled and wrestled its columned length before tumbling over the grill-work bannister onto the lawn.

Mrs. Dahlgren replaced her frown of disapproval with what she hoped was a countenance of composure (composure is not easy to achieve in a household with eleven children) before she returned to the parlor.

If Miss Percy had overheard the remarks in the hall, she gave no evidence of it. She had risen from the sofa and was standing across the room beside a harp.

"Who plays this harp?" she asked, running her fingers across the strings. She did talk "funny"; her native Mississippi drawl had a decided foreign accent, and her "funny smell" was the aroma of exotic perfume.

"Nobody plays the harp now. At least not often," Mrs. Dahlgren replied. "Mr. Dahlgren bought it for Sarah soon after we built Dunleith, hoping it would encourage her musical talents. She took lessons and learned to play rather well, but she never enjoyed the harp, and now she appears to have lost interest in it entirely."

"May I play?" Miss Percy asked.

"Please do!" Mrs. Dahlgren answered.

Miss Percy seated herself in a brocaded chair and drew the harp to her. She plucked the strings hesitantly at first, almost as though she feared a discordant rebuff from the instrument, but after a few minutes she began playing a rippling, sweet melody.

Mrs. Dahlgren did not recognize the tune, yet it seemed as familiar as lullabies she hummed to her children. As she listened, Mrs. Dahlgren decided that Miss Percy had composed the music as she played, drawing from the strings a song of love, of waiting, of rejection, of homesickness, of loneliness.

Mrs. Dahlgren brushed away a sudden trickle of tears.

Two grubby little boys stood spellbound and silent in the doorway.

And upstairs Sarah listened and wondered.

Why, Sarah wondered, had she never heard of her cousin, Miss Percy? Why had Miss Percy come to Dunleith? What story was the music telling?

Mr. Dahlgren, when he came home from his bank, provided no answers for Sarah's questions though he indicated that he, too, was interested in the length of Miss Percy's visit.

"She brought just one little trunk," Sarah told Mr. Dahlgren, "so she must not plan to visit long. It's an old trunk, battered and scratched, that looks as if it has been on a long journey."

"No doubt it has," Mr. Dahlgren remarked. He said nothing else, leaving Sarah to wonder if he knew where the trunk—and Miss Percy—had been.

Sarah questioned the servants, but she learned nothing from them, nor were her friends able to provide her with information about Miss Percy.

It was Miss Percy herself who, some weeks later, satisfied Sarah's curiosity—or some of it.

Sarah walked into the parlor one afternoon when Miss Percy was playing the harp. On this occasion, she was singing softly. Sarah listened and exclaimed,

"You're singing a French song!"

The music stopped, and Miss Percy looked inquiringly at Sarah. "Yes. I learned the song in Paris. Do you know it?" she asked.

Sarah did know the song (she had learned it during the months she studied in Europe), so together she and Miss Percy sang the French words.

As the song ended, Miss Percy placed her hand gently on Sarah's shoulder and said, "Thank you, my dear, for singing with me. It has been a long time since anyone has shared my music. I used to sing that song with someone I loved very much. He and I—"

Sarah leaned forward eagerly, impatient to hear what Miss Percy was about to say, but the greying lady stopped short, sighed and said only,

"But that was a long, long time ago."

Then Miss Percy rose and hurried upstairs to her room.

Sarah sat alone in the parlor, going over in her mind the things Miss Percy had said and puzzling over the things Miss Percy had not said. She was trying to imagine Miss Percy young and in love when Mrs. Dahlgren came into the room.

"Mother, who was Miss Percy in love with?" Sarah asked.

"Miss Percy? In love? I—I really do not know his name."

Actually Mrs. Dahlgren was telling the truth: she did not recall the name of Miss Percy's lover. She—Mrs. Dahlgren— and others in Natchez who knew the story always referred to the man in Miss Percy's life as "that Frenchman."

Some older residents of the river town said the man was a French count or duke. Others contended that he was a high-ranking officer in the French Army. Whatever his title or rank, he had accompanied Prince Louis Philippe (later to serve as King of France from 1830 to 1848) on a visit to Natchez in the early 1800s.

During the stay of the royal entourage in Natchez, Miss Percy met and fell in love with "that Frenchman." Their love affair was the talk of Natchez, and even Prince Louis Philippe is said to have taken an interest in their romance, referring to them as "that charmingly happy couple."

The two, Miss Percy and "that Frenchman," were not

66

married during the foreigners' stay in Natchez nor was there an official announcement of their engagement, but he is supposed to have promised to send for Miss Percy as soon as conditions in unsettled France made it possible for her to join him there.

So Miss Percy waited. Months passed with no word from "that Frenchman." Then, when everyone except Miss Percy had concluded that the love affair was a mere flirtation and that the French visitor had never intended to send for Miss Percy, the letter arrived. Miss Percy shared its contents with no one, but its message made her ecstatically happy.

A week later she had packed a small trunk and had gone to New Orleans where she boarded a ship bound for France. Everyone in Natchez assumed, of course, that Miss Percy had gone to marry "that Frenchman," and they were delighted with this happy ending to a storybook romance.

Truthfully, not everybody was happy about Miss Percy's trip to France. Certain members of her family considered the journey entirely improper. No properly-reared young lady, they contended, went traipsing off without a chaperone to join a man who was not yet her husband. People close to the family said some of the Percys even told Miss Percy that the Frenchman would never marry her. There were, reportedly, heated words exchanged and ultimatums issued by older male members of the family.

Although this family unpleasantness may have cast a slight gloom over Miss Percy's departure, it did not for one minute lessen her determination to cross the ocean and join the man she loved.

Because they knew Paris is a long way from Natchez and they were aware that communications between the two points were chancey, Miss Percy's friends were not disturbed when they did not hear from her. At first they thought she was too excited and too busy preparing for her wedding to write. Later they decided perhaps she had been changed by her life as a member of the French court and that she no longer cared for her former friends.

"She has forgotten all about us," they said.

And, after awhile, they forgot about her. Or most of them did.

Unfortunately, Miss Percy's life in France was neither glamorous nor exciting. Nothing turned out the way she had thought it would. Her lover, so attentive and considerate in Natchez, became increasingly indifferent and surly in his native France.

At first he had seemed overjoyed to have her with him again. They explored the countryside together; they attended balls at court; they entertained small groups of his friends with their music, he singing to the accompaniment of her harp; they visited art museums and attended concerts; and they purchased clothes for her in shops more elegant than Miss Percy had ever imagined.

But they did not marry.

Always, it seemed, he found excuses for postponing the wedding plans. After awhile, he even refused to discuss marriage, and finally he told her,

"I no longer find you amusing or entertaining. I wish you had never come to France!"

Just how long it was before this final rejection came or how long she tried to reclaim his affections, no one in Natchez ever knew, but it was some years after her departure that Miss Percy quietly returned to Natchez.

Embarrassed to face her family, to hear their, "I-told-you-sos," Miss Percy turned to Mrs. Dahlgren, to whom she was connected by marriage, for comfort and for shelter.

In the Dahlgrens' imposing new home, Dunleith, showplace of Natchez, Miss Percy found refuge from prying eyes and gossiping tongues. There, too, she found solace in music.

She never left the house, but each afternoon she went downstairs to play the harp. The swish of her full skirts as she descended the stairs announced the daily concert, and often members of the family or servants would slip into the parlor to listen to her plaintive music. Playing the harp was her sole interest for only in her music could she recapture the happiness she had once known or pour out the burden of a broken heart.

For Miss Percy's heart was broken. She still loved "that Frenchman," still longed to be with him.

If it is true that people can die of broken hearts, that is what happened to Miss Percy. One afternoon she failed to come swishing down the stairs to play the harp. When Mrs. Dahlgren went to see what had detained her, she found Miss Percy sitting motionless in a low rocking chair by the window. The doctor, who was quickly summoned, said she had been dead for several hours.

A few days after Miss Percy's funeral, Sarah walked into the hall and heard, coming from the parlor, the familiar strains of the duet she and Miss Percy had sung. She rushed into the parlor to see who was playing the harp, but as she entered the room, the music stopped.

No one was there.

"Mother!" Sarah called, "I was sure I heard Miss Percy playing, but...."

"Yes, dear," her mother replied, "I heard her harp music, too."

That was the first of the ghostly late afternoon concerts Miss Percy gave on the haunted harp. For more than a century those concerts have continued. Residents of Dunleith still hear the swishing of long skirts followed by plaintive

Miss Percy played the harp to recapture her lost happiness and unburden her broken heart.

melodies from a harp as Miss Percy releases in music her love and her longing for "that Frenchman."

Miss Percy came to Dunleith for a long, long visit.

Castalian Springs three miles west of Durant.

The General

Nobody could tell finer ghost stories than Joe Paslay.

Year after year YMCA campers at Castalian Springs heard Paslay, the camp director, tell ghost stories, and they all agreed he was a real expert.

"Mr. Paslay could even scare you in the daytime," a former camper recalls.

Paslay and his staff created a fearsome cast of ghostly characters: headless horsemen (no camp should be without one), Indian braves, vampires, Confederate soldiers, ruthless bandits. With each telling, they embroidered upon the escapades of these spirits, adding terrifying episodes as the situations required.

Paslay, of course, did not believe in ghosts. He never intentionally frightened campers with his tales either: on those rare occasions when a child really got scared, Paslay calmly assured him that the stories were all made up—not true at all—and that there were no such things as ghosts.

That was before Joe Paslay met The General.

Their meeting occurred during the summer of 1961. Paslay had living quarters (three connecting rooms along a long hall) between the recreation room and the dining room in the rambling frame building that served as headquarters for camp activities. His apartment was not plush, but it provided the most comfortable sleeping accommodations at camp.

One night YMCA officials from Jackson came for an overnight stay at Castalian Springs, and, since there were no guest quarters, Paslay let them occupy his apartment.

There were several empty rooms on the second floor, and Paslay moved into one of them for the night. After he made sure that the visitors were comfortable, he went upstairs and got ready for bed.

The heavy summer heat clung to the upstairs room. Paslay shoved the curtains back from the upstairs windows and left his door wide open, hoping a breeze would clear away the sultry stuffiness. He was not sleepy, so he picked up a book and read in bed for two hours or more, much longer than he had intended to. It was nearly 1:00 a.m. when he closed the book and turned out his light. The building was quiet; everyone else was asleep.

Seconds later, Paslay saw someone standing in the door of his room. A light left burning in a bathroom down the hall provided just enough illumination to outline the figure in the doorway, a figure wearing a flowing cape.

Paslay waited for his visitor to speak, but he said nothing.

"What do you want? Is anything wrong?" Paslay asked.

As soon as Paslay spoke, the figure vanished.

Paslay jumped out of bed and ran to the door. The long hall was empty and silent. A quick—and thorough—check of the building gave no clue as to who his visitor might have been. Everyone was sound asleep, and the doors leading outside were all still locked.

Paslay returned to his second floor room. He was too excited and puzzled to sleep, and he needed to share his

75

experience with someone. At the far end of the upstairs hall two counsellors, Nita Fonville of Tchula and Carol Watters of Collierville, Tennessee, shared a room, the only other room on the floor occupied at the time. Paslay went to their door and knocked until he waked them.

"Who is it?" Nina asked sleepily.

"It's me—Joe Paslay. I just wondered if you all heard anybody walking around up here a few minutes ago."

"No. We haven't heard anything," Carol replied. "We've been asleep a long time. Nobody has been down at this end of the hall. Is anything wrong, Mr. Paslay?"

Though Paslay wanted desperately to discuss his experience with someone, he did not want to alarm the girls, so he answered, "Everything is all right. I—I just thought somebody had come up here looking for me. See you in the morning."

He was tempted to add, "I've just seen a ghost," but he did not.

When he went back to bed, Paslay lay for a long time thinking about what he had seen. He was certain, absolutely sure, that he had seen a figure standing in his doorway, a rather tall person, bareheaded and wearing a military-type cape.

The more he thought about it, the more convinced Paslay became that his visitor was a soldier, not a modern-day warrior but a soldier from the past. Paslay even gave the apparition a name: he called him The General.

Paslay had directed the Castalian Springs camp for several summers, and he was rather familiar with the history of the place. He recalled, lying there in the dark, that Confederate soldiers had been quartered on the site. He had often taken campers on hikes to a small, neglected cemetery where unknown Confederate dead are buried.

Could his silent visitor have been one of those unknown dead? Paslay finally fell asleep, still wondering.

Next day Paslay told of his experience, not to campers (he had no wish to upset them) but to mature members of his staff. He had expected to be teased, but most of the people to whom he told his story listened with interest and concern. They had been associated with him long enough to know that Joe Paslay was completely honest and that, furthermore, he was not the kind of man who would let his imagination play tricks on him. They agreed, almost unanimously, that if Joe Paslay said a Confederate general visited his room, a Confederate general did indeed visit him.

As soon as he could find a Mississippi history book, Paslay refreshed his memory about the role of Castalian Springs in the War Between the States. He found that the Confederate States of America requisitioned the property (it had been a boarding school for "young ladies of fine character and family") for use as a hospital.

It was to Castalian Springs that some of the survivors of Shiloh were brought in April, 1862. After that battle, the living were picked from among the dead bodies sprawled beneath the splintered peach trees, were dumped into farm wagons like bloody bags of grain, and were hauled away. Some, the fortunate, were taken to first aid stations and emergency hospitals nearby, but many of the wounded were jolted and bumped across Mississippi for two hundred miles or so before they received medical treatment.

Paslay never learned exactly how many wounded were hauled to Castalian Springs, but he did learn that at least forty-three of them died. They were buried on a wooded knoll, close beside the road, about a mile from the springs. Each grave was marked with a wooden slab.

Those burials were made a long time ago. The road has long been abandoned, and trees grow where wagon wheels once rolled. The grave markers rotted. A century of rain and wind wore away the rows of rectangular earth mounds.

Now a sagging wire fence encloses a stone shaft on which is engraved:

To the Memory of the Confederate Soldiers of Kentucky, Tennessee and Missouri—Love's Last Tribute—Erected by the Holmes County Camp No. 389 U.C.V. and Others—Confederate Soldiers Sent to Castalian Springs Hospital from Shiloh, April, 1862.

When he next visited that solitary shaft, Paslay kicked aside crumpled potato chip bags, rusty beer cans, and cigarette packages left by earlier visitors, and he determined to dispatch a squad of campers to clean up the area. He read the inscription, and he wondered where The General was from. Was he a Tennesseean? A Kentuckian? From Missouri?

Most of all Paslay wondered if The General would come to Castalian Springs again.

He did come back, several times, but he never appeared to Joe Paslay again.

"Always," Paslay says, "The General would appear on the second floor of the old building, the part where I was the night I saw him. He seemed to feel that the second floor belongs to him, and he seemed to resent what he considered our intrusion on his private property or into his quarters."

There was the occasion in 1967, Paslay recalls, when David Gandy, a counsellor from Hattiesburg, was in bed on the second floor. David was a sophomore in college at the time. The lights were out, and David was wondering why his roommate, Andy Blackwell, had not come up to bed.

David was about to get up and go look for Andy when someone came in and sat on the foot of his bed. Thinking it was Andy, David began fussing at him, asking where he had been so late.

There was no reply.

David sat up in bed to berate Andy for his rudeness

When he did, the figure on the foot of the bed vanished. Nobody was there.

Nobody was in the hall either or in any of the nearby rooms.

David—and Andy—were relieved when that camp session ended.

That same summer, according to Paslay, another counsellor, also named David, had an encounter with The General. This David was a brawny fellow, a football star at Mississippi State. He had never been frightened by anything in his life until the night he was awakened by strange noises and saw the ghostly figure of a man moving about in his upstairs room.

David moved out and left the premises completely in command of The General.

"There were other encounters, other visits from The General," Paslay recalls. "Strange things, things which nobody could explain, continued to happen on that second floor. We blamed them all on The General. Several people— reliable staff members—reported seeing a tall figure wearing a flowing cape stride down the hall or appear unannounced in a room. That second floor was haunted."

The Mississippi YMCA has closed Castalian Springs camp and has sold the property, not because of The General's visitations but for financial reasons.

Joe Paslay, who lives in Durant, still tells ghost stories occasionally, but he does not tell the made-up kind. He tells a true story about the night The General called on him at Castalian Springs.

Anchuca now stands in Vicksburg.

The Rebellious Miss Archer

Richard T. Archer had an inquiring mind.

When he was growing up in Amelia Court House, Virginia, he read every book in the town, maybe not every one, but he did read more than any other boy in the county. And he was always wanting to try things out, to experiment.

He built all sorts of things, from models of Eli Whitney's cotton gin to folding stands for his mother's potted plants. Every time he read about something new, he wanted to try it. Neighbors recalled that Richard dammed up creeks to see how locks could raise and lower the toy boats he made; built replicas of the Roman aqueducts; fashioned musical instruments; usurped part of the garden for his beehives so he could study flight patterns of bees; kept accurate records of weather; and came very near constructing a perpetual motion machine.

By the time he was sent to Pennsylvania to college, his head was already so filled with learning, neighbors said, that it seemed a waste to send him off to get more schooling.

It was while he was in Pennsylvania that Richard Archer met Ann Barnes. Ann, an orphan, was attending school in

81

Philadelphia. The young students fell in love, married, and moved to Mississippi where the Archer family was then living.

Richard began planting in Claiborne County, learning from older and more experienced planters how to operate a large plantation and to supervise all the supportive operations such a venture required.

In 1837 Ann and Richard moved from Oaken Grove Plantation, the home of Mr. and Mrs. Stephen C. Archer, to a home of their own near Port Gibson. They called their home Anchuca.

Richard Archer's craftsmanship and attention to details were reflected in the fine home he built. It was a two-and-one-half story house with wide halls, spacious rooms, and shady porches. The ceilings were decorated with frescoes from patterns designed by Mr. Archer, and the millwork throughout the house was of a quality which prompted envy and admiration.

Cedar trees, set out with geometrical precision, outlined the curving approaches to Anchuca. Mr. Archer planned the landscaping of the grounds himself, and he planted there many unusual and colorful shrubs and flowers.

Mr. Archer knew the scientific name of every growing thing he planted, just as he knew the proper architectural term to describe every feature of his house. He shared this information with his children—there were nine of them—but none of the young Archers (with the exception of a daughter) was interested in such matters. They admired and respected him and wondered how he could possibly carry so much diversified knowledge around in his head, but occasionally his unconventional projects caused them considerable embarrassment.

There was, for instance, the episode with the pond.

Soon after he built his house, Richard Archer selected a spot not far away where he constructed a large pond. The pond was fed by a meandering branch, and trees along its banks provided shade for fishermen and for strollers. It was a favorite gathering place for the family and for their guests.

Mr. Archer made business trips to New Orleans occasionally, and he delighted in visiting that port city. There were books in New Orleans and people who had read them, people with whom he could discuss theories, science, theology, and philosophy. Always he returned from New Orleans with bundles of books for his library and stimulating ideas for his mind.

One of the things he enjoyed most in New Orleans was dining on fresh seafood. He particularly liked oysters.

On one of those business trips, Mr. Archer was savoring a big platter of raw oysters in one of New Orleans' fine restaurants when an idea came to him. Why not, he asked himself, raise oysters in the pond at Anchuca?

With his own oysters in his own pond just below his own house, he could have the delicacy served any time he chose. Mr. Archer was almost jubilant over the idea, and he immediately set in motion plans to carry it out.

He knew that oysters grow only in salt water, so he ordered barrels of salt (he figured how many he would need by means of a complicated equation of his own devising) shipped to Anchuca. He also had barrels of oysters shipped to his plantation. He supervised the packing of the oysters so that each barrel would contain enough salt water to keep the oysters alive and healthy during the trip.

On the day the salt and the oysters arrived, neighbors from miles around converged on Anchuca to watch Richard Archer's slaves plant the oysters.

Mr. Archer stationed slaves with long poles around the edges of the pond to stir and agitate the water as the salt was poured in. Other slaves in skiffs and on rafts out in the middle of the pond stirred and beat the water with poles and paddles to dissolve and distribute the salt.

When Mr. Archer considered the water sufficiently salty (he tested it frequently), he ordered the slaves to open the barrels and dump the oysters into the pond.

"Before long now, we'll be having an oyster supper with plenty of oysters, fresh from my own pond, for everybody," Mr. Archer told his neighbors.

Things did not work out that way.

Several days after the oysters were placed in the pond, it became evident that something was wrong. There was a definite odor, faint but disagreeable, hovering about the water. The next day, the smell was definitely worse, and before the week was out, the stench was unbearable.

Mr. Archer moved his family to the Planters Hotel in nearby Port Gibson where they took up residence for several weeks as refugees from the oyster experiment.

They took a lot of teasing, of course, especially Mr. Archer, about the demise of the oysters. He took the joking good-naturedly. Actually, he did not really listen to it: he was already cogitating about a plan for converting native gum trees into mahogany by boring holes at intervals in the trunks of the trees and filling the holes with heavy oil.

He was worried, too, about his daughter, the one who looked so much like him that her family nickname was Archie. A nurse, amused by the resemblance of daughter to father, had called the baby Archie soon after she was born, and the name stuck. Richard Archer did not particularly like such a masculine name, even though it was a pet nickname, for such a delightfully feminine girl though it did please him that even strangers noticed how much he and his daughter looked alike.

Mr. Archer loved each of his five daughters, took pride in their beauty and in their accomplishments, but there was something special about his relationship with Archie. In addition to looking alike, they shared many of the same interests: she read almost as many of the books he brought home from New Orleans as he did, and she encouraged some of his unorthodox experiments. They, Mr. Archer and Archie, were equally headstrong and stubborn.

Mr. Archer particularly enjoyed his conversations with Archie around the family table at mealtime. With other family members adding comments and personal opinions, he and Archie discussed and debated an array of topics, matching wits and knowledge and having a fine time.

But now Mr. Archer was worried about Archie. He had seen some indications that she was attracted by—he refused to think it could be more than a foolish attraction—Josh Melvin, the son of Mr. Archer's overseer. Josh was a nice enough young man—Mr. Archer had never heard anything against him—but he was the overseer's son. As such he was not socially acceptable as a suitor or even as a companion for the daughter of the plantation owner. Archie understood this code of behavior, Mr. Archer told himself. He hoped he would not have to remind her of it.

Then he chided himself for even thinking there could be anything serious between his Archie and Josh Melvin. He was probably imagining the whole thing, he told himself. But he kept remembering a glance he saw Archie and Josh exchange the morning the barrels of oysters had been emptied into the pond. He recalled, too, that Josh often appeared at Anchuca on some vague errand and that it was always Archie who met him on the porch.

He had seen Archie smiling up at Josh and laughing at something the youth had told her when he—Mr. Archer—had come out onto the porch one afternoon. He should have spoken to Archie about her behavior then, but he did not want to magnify what he hoped was a trivial indiscretion. He had no wish to quarrel with Archie. Immediately he wondered why he assumed there would be a quarrel: he and Archie had never had cross words. It was probably nothing. All fathers worry about their daughters.

But Mr. Archer continued to be troubled.

He noticed, during their stay at Port Gibson, that Archie seemed bored by the young men who came calling. He noticed, too, that she invented many excuses for riding out to Anchuca. Almost every day she developed an urgent need for some item from home: a book, a particular ribbon for her hair, a hymnal, a piece of jewelry, embroidery thread, a chemise, water colors, or some other such trifle.

The distance between Port Gibson and Anchuca was only two miles, and Archie's maid always accompanied her on the short journeys. They were never gone long. But Mr. Archer kept being tormented by the knowledge that Josh was out at the plantation helping his father supervise the draining and cleaning of what some Port Gibson wits were calling "the oyster bowl."

One afternoon, lashed by his suspicions, Mr. Archer followed his daughter shortly after she left on an apparently impulsive ride out to Anchuca. Mr. Archer took a back road, cutting across cotton fields and through a patch of woods. He rode near the pond and noticed that the odor was nearly gone. He was grateful for he was homesick for Anchuca and wanted to move home again.

Mr. Archer tied his horse behind a cotton shed and walked toward the house. He hated himself for spying on his daughter—but he had to know.

Then he saw them.

Archie and Josh were sitting on a bench beneath a tall cedar. They were so absorbed in conversation that they did not notice Mr. Archer's approach.

"Josh Melvin, get off my land," Mr. Archer ordered. "Now!" His voice was hard and cold, shaking with anger.

Josh rose quickly and faced Mr. Archer. "Sir," he said, "we have done nothing wrong. I love your daughter. We would like your permission to be married. We—"

Mr. Archer struck Josh hard across his face with a riding crop.

"Go!"

Josh started toward the older man, but Archie grabbed his arm. "Please, Josh. Please go," she begged. "I'll talk to Father. Please go."

Josh turned and walked away.

"So you have been meeting that white trash behind my back," Mr. Archer stormed. "My own daughter meeting the son of my overseer!"

"Father!" Archie shouted, "I will not let you talk about Josh like that. I love him, and I intend to marry him!"

"Never!" her father replied. "Never! I will see that his father sends him away."

Archie looked straight at her father as she said slowly, "If you send Josh away, I will never again eat a meal at your table." Then she mounted her horse and rode back to Port Gibson.

The Archer family returned to Anchuca the following day. The faint odor of spoiled oysters remained, but nobody mentioned it, and the household gradually settled back into its usual routine.

One thing changed though: Archie did not join the family at the table at mealtime.

Richard Archer, carrying out his threat, had seen that Josh was sent away. Such things could be arranged. Archie, carrying out her threat, never sat down to a meal with her family at Anchuca again.

For as long as she lived at Anchuca, the headstrong girl had all her meals served in the parlor where she stood beside the fireplace and ate from the marble mantel.

Richard Archer died in 1867.

Many years later, Anchuca was purchased by a resident of Vicksburg, was dismantled, moved, and reassembled on Rifle Range Road in that city.

In 1966, Mr. and Mrs. Jack Lavender and their family moved into the house. They knew little of its history, but they liked its spaciousness and appreciated its workmanship.

One day their daughter Mel walked into the parlor and saw the figure of a young girl standing by the mantel. The ghostly girl, Mel remembers, seemed to be about eighteen years old, was quite pretty and was wearing a long brown dress.

Mel was startled but not frightened. She stood in the doorway and gazed at the figure until it slowly faded away. Then Mel immediately told her parents of the experience, describing each detail of the strange encounter and adding, "I felt sorry for her somehow."

That was the first of several times the ghost of the brown-clad girl was seen standing by the mantel, the same mantel from which Archie ate so many meals in the old Archer home.

Mel Lavender was, naturally, interested in the ghost she had seen and tried to find out who the apparition could be, but no one she asked knew the history of the Archer family.

Harry, the Lavender's butler, wanted to know the identity of the ghost, too: he met her frequently when he went into the basement on errands.

It was five years or more after she first saw the ghost in the parlor of her home that Mel heard the story of Archie Archer's vow never to sit at the family table and of her stubborn insistence on dining from the mantel.

Mel is sure, just as other people who know of the events are sure, that she saw the unhappy ghost of Archie Archer, still stubborn and still defiant. And still lonely.

Judge William Lake home in Vicksburg.

The Lovely Afternoon

Judge William Lake had taken his short afternoon nap, a custom of long standing with the Vicksburg jurist. He slipped on his coat, straightened his vest, and, after a few moments of searching, called,

"My dear, do you know where my glasses are?"

Mrs. Lake came into the bedroom where her husband had been resting. She walked unerringly to the tall dresser, picked up the glasses, and handed them to the judge.

"Thank you," he said. "I could not remember where I had laid them."

Mrs. Lake wondered, as she had wondered every afternoon for a quarter of a century, how a man who could recall every legal detail of a complicated civil case could never remember where he had put his glasses. The glasses were always in the same place, always on the dresser, but always the judge summoned help to find them. The search for the glasses was as much a part of his daily routine as was his habit of rising from the dinner table and, after complimenting the quality of the heavy midday meal, announcing as though he were about to take some new and startling course of action,

"I believe I'll take a little nap before I go back to the office."

"Do, dear," she always replied. "I'm sure you need a little rest." She always used the same words.

During the half hour or so between the time the judge announced his intention of taking a nap and the time he called for assistance in finding his glasses, the house at the corner of Main and Adams was abnormally quiet: no doors slammed, all conversation was in whispers, all walking was on tiptoe. Only the clock in the upstairs sitting room continued its normal routine, and it was the sonorous striking of this timepiece that roused Judge Lake from his sleep.

This day Judge Lake, ready to return to his book-lined office, paused to bid his wife good-bye, just as he always did.

"Good-bye, my dear. Have a lovely afternoon."

They were the words he always said, but this afternoon they sounded a bit different, a bit hoarse or husky. Mrs. Lake noticed the difference, slight though it was, and asked quickly,

"Are you all right? Is anything wrong?"

He cleared his throat. "No. No—nothing is wrong. Good-bye, my dear. Have a lovely afternoon."

He kissed her lightly and walked out into the October afternoon.

It was, to all appearances, a farewell like thousands of others on thousands of other afternoons, but Judge William Lake knew it was different: this afternoon he was not returning to his office. He was going to fight a duel.

He wanted to look back, wanted to see again the way his house looked with the autumn sun shining on its galleries and balconies and gardens, but he was afraid his wife might be watching and might wonder at the gesture. She had caught a hint of something unusual in his farewell, and he did not wish to arouse her anxiety. He was pleased that he had been able to hide his own apprehension from her by following without deviation his normal routine.

He did not want Mrs. Lake to worry, did not want to spoil her afternoon. He remembered, walking down the steep hill toward his office, how she always delighted in her afternoons. Usually, after he returned to work, she rested and read a bit before dressing for the afternoon. Sometimes she went calling, riding in her carriage over the bumpy streets, to the homes of friends, and sometimes she entertained at her own home where she served her guests tiny beaten biscuits with quince jelly or dainty sandwiches or French pastries. He teased her about her fancy tea parties and laughed in amusement at the tid-bits of gossip ("crumbs from the party," he called them) which she passed along to him.

Every afternoon, weather permitting, she walked in her garden. She cut fresh flowers for the house, and she gave instructions to the gardener about planting, pruning, and cultivating the flowers and shrubs. Already, though several weeks of lingering summer warmth remained, they were making plans to move the tender plants—begonias, elephant ears, sultanas, and ferns—to the deep flower pit for the winter.

Mrs. Lake reveled in the beauty of her garden. "It restoreth my soul," she used to say, and in times of trouble she sought solace there.

Lately, Judge Lake recalled, she had had less time for her garden. She had been busy with war work: embroidering battle flags, knitting, writing letters, preparing hospital kits and such. It was a war year, 1861, and the South, the Confederate States of America, was engaged in bitter combat with Union forces.

Mrs. Lake's conscience bothered her when she spent time in her garden instead of devoting her full energies to supporting "our gallant men in grey," but Judge Lake encouraged her to continue her strolls in the garden. He understood her need for the renewal which the garden provided.

Wherever she went during her afternoons, Mrs. Lake always left a lingering, gentle fragrance of haunting sweetness. For years, since Judge Lake brought her the first tiny bottle, she had used the same kind of perfume, a delicate and elusive blend of floral scents. Perhaps jasmine predominated. It was difficult to tell.

Judge Lake, that October afternoon, half fancied that the fragrance of his wife's perfume followed him along the sidewalk. It was a foolish fancy, of course. How much of the perfume did she have on her dressing table, he wondered. He tried to recall whether or not he had brought her a bottle when he returned from his last trip to New Orleans, but he could not. He hoped he had.

He passed the new courthouse, its columned porticos and tall cupola towering over Vicksburg, and he wondered if he would ever again appear in a courtroom there.

"I must not think such morbid thoughts," he reprimanded himself.

But memories kept rushing in, demanding recognition.

He passed the corner where, as a young lawyer newly come to Vicksburg from Maryland, he had seen placards posted ordering the gamblers to leave town within twenty-four hours. That had been an exciting time. Even now he recalled vividly—had it really been a quarter of a century ago?—details of the episode and the feelings of tension that gripped the town.

He remembered the Fourth of July celebration which had been disrupted by the vulgar behavior of a gambler, a man named Cabler, who had come uninvited to the social affair. Cabler was ejected, but he returned later armed with loaded pistol, knife, and dagger and vowed to kill the gentleman who had ousted him.

Cabler's vow of revenge was never carried out: he was taken into custody by a group of citizens, responsible men, who took him into the nearby woods where they lashed him, applied a covering of tar and feathers to his body, and ordered him out of town.

Encouraged by their success in ridding Vicksburg of one of its evil leeches, civic leaders called a public meeting to make plans for ousting all professional gamblers from their dens along the river. The law-abiding townspeople could no longer tolerate the gamblers' insolence, vulgarity, insults, thievery, and brutality.

The plan agreed upon was to inform the gamblers that they had twenty-four hours to get out of Vicksburg. Vigilantes would rout out any who defied the order.

Judge Lake had sharp recollections of that July morning in 1835 when a posse of citizens advanced on the house where five of the most notorious gambling sharks had barricaded themselves. In the brief skirmish there, Dr. Hugh Bodley, a young and beloved physician, was killed by a shot from the house. Enraged by the death of their friend, the Vicksburg vigilantes stormed the structure and took five men (Dutch Bill, Smith, McCall, North, and Hullums) into custody.

A short time later, five bodies dangled from five taut ropes.

Judge Lake recalled distinctly the tone of terrified disbelief in the voice of North when he cried out,

"In the name of God, gentlemen, surely you are not going to hang us!"

The sigh of a tightened noose was his reply.

The judge remembered, too, how on the following day the five bodies were cut down and buried in a ditch.

"If death comes to me today," he thought, "at least I

will be accorded a decent burial."

Again he upbraided himself for harbouring morbid thoughts.

Truthfully, Judge Lake did feel morbid. He dreaded the duel he faced. Unlike many of his friends, he found no glory or pride in defending his honor on a private field of battle, and he secretly decried the punctilious code of conduct that demanded such action.

He had no desire to kill Mr. Chambers, his adversary. Mr. Chambers was his political opponent in a contest for a seat in the Confederate Congress, but, though the canvass was heatedly partisan, Judge Lake had no personal enmity toward the man. Certainly he did not want to kill him. Yet somehow he had become involved in a situation that, according to the code of a gentleman's behavior, could only be settled by engaging in a duel.

The challenge had been issued and accepted; the seconds had been named; the site and time and weapons (pistols at ten paces) had been agreed upon; and the surgeons had been notified to be present, all according to the precise and formal pattern required by the code duello.

How, Judge Lake wondered, had he allowed himself to be caught in the trap of senseless medieval chivalry? He was fifty-three years old, and he did not want to kill or to be killed.

Yet already across the river on De Soto Point, seconds were making final arrangements for the duel. The sandy strip of land had been agreed upon as the site because of its strategic location. It was beyond the Mississippi boundary and therefore immune from interference by law officers from that state (dueling was illegal), and it was so far removed from any Louisiana town that arrest by Louisiana officers was highly unlikely. The Point had become a favorite dueling ground.

Plans called for the two adversaries, their seconds, and their surgeons to cross the river in separate boats and to meet at the Point for final instructions. Other boats were already crossing the stream as spectators gathered to watch the affray, and considerable money was being wagered on its outcome.

From the beginning, from the issuance of the challenge until that very day, Judge Lake's primary concern had been the fear that his wife would learn of the duel. She, gentle and sensitive, could never have understood the necessity for mortal combat (how could he explain it to her when he himself could not justify it?), and the knowledge that her husband faced a duel would have caused her deep heartache, deeper than her garden could restore.

So Judge Lake had taken every precaution to keep the news of the duel from his wife. And on this afternoon, this lovely afternoon, as he walked toward the waiting boat, his only consolation was that she had been spared the sad knowledge of his involvement in a duel.

But she did know.

Mrs. Lake, after the judge had left the house, had rested a bit, and had then begun to dress for the afternoon. She had put on a silk dress (she loved the swishing rustle of the full skirt, and it rather amused her that she, a middle-aged married woman, should still find pleasure in such girlish trivialities), and she was touching perfume to her throat, her temples, and her wrists when her maid burst into the room.

"Missus—It's bad news! The Judge is going to fight! He's on his way across the river. It's that man—Mr. Chambers—"

Mrs. Lake whirled around from the dressing table and demanded, "What are you saying?"

As she started across the room toward the distraught woman, Mrs. Lake knocked over the bottle of perfume, and it spilled over on the dresser, ran down the sides and formed

97

a tiny puddle on the pine floor.

"What are you saying?" Mrs. Lake demanded again.

The maid was too upset to reply immediately, but under Mrs. Lake's prodding she repeated her story. Word of the impending duel had come from the home of one of the seconds where a butler had heard it discussed by gentlemen enjoying their after-dinner drinks and cigars. The butler had told the cook who had passed the news along to the gardener who had whispered it to a maid down the street who had hurried to the Lake's servants' quarters with the tidings.

"I had to tell you," the maid sobbed. "How we go' stop him? Judge Lake ain't no fighter—he be killed sho'!"

"Hush!" Mrs. Lake snapped. "You're not to talk that way! Bring my opera glasses and come with me."

Perhaps, Mrs. Lake told herself as the two women climbed the stairs to the second floor of the house, the story was not true. Surely Judge Lake would have told her if he were going to fight a duel. But, deep in her heart, she knew he would have tried to spare her worry and grief, that he would say, just as he had said, "Have a lovely afternoon, my dear."

Still, the servants may have misunderstood, may have been mistaken.

Mrs. Lake, followed by her maid, went out onto the second floor verandah where they had a clear view of the river and of De Soto Point on the other side.

Even without the opera glasses, Mrs. Lake could see an unusually large number of boats crossing the river to the Point, and when she trained her glasses on the Point, she saw a crowd of men gathered there. She moved the glasses slowly from group to group, fearing to find a familiar figure.

Then she saw him. At the edge of the gathering, in close conversation with a man whom she also recognized, was her husband.

Mrs. Lake stood on the high porch and watched in silence as the second loaded a pistol and handed it to Judge Lake. She saw Judge Lake and Mister Chambers stand back to back, then step off the prescribed distance. She saw the white handkerchief drop, and she saw the twin puffs of smoke when the pistols were fired.

The smoke cleared. Judge Lake lay on the ground.

"O, God!" Mrs. Lake breathed. "O, God!"

"Come on, Missus. Let's go downstairs," the maid urged. "Don't look no mo'. Please don't look no mo'."

But Mrs. Lake could not move. She stood as though hypnotized with her glasses focused on the tragic scene across the river. She watched the surgeon kneel on the sand to examine Judge Lake, saw him rise, and shake his head. She saw the seconds lift Judge Lake's body and place it in a boat.

As the craft started across the river, she dropped her glasses and walked slowly downstairs.

It was more than a century ago that Mrs. Lake stood on the upstairs gallery that lovely afternoon and watched her husband's death.

The house is still there in Vicksburg at the corner of Main and Adams. The top story, where the ballroom and the guest bedrooms and the gallery with the view of the river were located, was destroyed by fire in 1916, but the lower floor retains its original design and charm.

The house has been restored by its present owner, John Wayne Jabour, a young Vicksburg businessman, who purchased the property in 1973 from the heirs of B. Coccaro, a grocer, who had acquired the place about 1900.

A few residents of the old Lake home have seen a shadowy figure strolling in the garden along the worn paths Mrs. Lake followed when she sought solace there, when she needed to restore her soul.

And each generation of occupants of the house has told of hearing, on lovely afternoons, the swish of silk skirts along the porch and in the garden and of smelling the tantalizing odor of exotic perfume, a haunting scent of flowers—jasmine, perhaps—such as Mrs. Lake used on lovely afternoons.

Waverley about six miles from Columbus.

Little Girl Lost

Sometimes when Mrs. Robert Snow is conducting visitors on a tour of her spectacular home, Waverley, she is tempted to say,

"And here in this upstairs bedroom is where our ghost—the ghost of a little girl—used to take her naps."

Instead she tells about the tall tester bed with its hand-carved posts, the decorative iron lining in the fireplace, and other features of the big room.

Though she does not mention the ghost of the little girl who haunts Waverley, Mrs. Snow does glance quickly at the bed each time she enters the room: she looks to see if it has been rumpled by a weary child, a ghost child.

The ghost came to Waverley about two years after Mr. and Mrs. Robert Allen Snow, Jr., bought the abandoned showplace in 1962, and though the spirit has made no manifestation of her presence for several years, Mrs. Snow keeps hoping she will come back home.

Waverley itself, the house, haunted Mr. and Mrs. Snow before they ever saw the fine old place.

A stranger walked into their antique shop in Philadelphia, Mississippi, one day and described to them "the grandest, most majestic house I ever saw."

The house, the man said, was somewhere along the Tombigbee River between West Point and Columbus. He had come upon it, quite by accident, years before, and even then it was bearing the signs of neglect that houses show when people desert them and condemn them to loneliness.

"I doubt that there's anything left there now," the stranger said. "Some bricks and rotting timber, maybe. The house is probably gone: it was years ago when I saw it. But what a place it was!"

He talked of the massiveness of the structure ("You wouldn't believe how big it was!"), of the graceful columns, the iron grillwork, the marble steps leading to the recessed porches, but it was his description of the house's soaring rotunda that captured the Snows' fancy.

"You walk into this huge entrance hall—big as a ball-room, and I guess maybe that was what it was—and you look up, and there is this octagonal balcony all the way around the sides of the big hall. No supports or anything. Then above that, there's another balcony just like it, and then another balcony above that. Three balconies circling that tremendous room!

"Then you keep looking up and there's the cupola, all decorated with plasterwork, fifty-five or sixty feet—maybe more—up over your head. And that's not all: there's a chandelier hanging down all the way from that high cupola to the middle of the ballroom.

"It's hard to believe that there's a house like that sitting vacant out there in the woods. Or there was. As I said, it has been years since I saw it. It's probably gone now."

After the man had left their shop, Mr. and Mrs. Snow talked about the house and wondered about it, wondering if any structure could be as magnificent as their customer had

One of the main entrance doors at Waverley.

pictured it. They could not forget his description of the house; they kept thinking of the sweeping rotunda with its three tiers of cantilevered balconies and of the cupola that soared maybe sixty feet straight up. One day Mr. Snow said,

"I've got to go look for that house. I can't get it out of my mind, and I must find out if it is still standing."

So the Snows went house-hunting.

They drove to the Columbus—West Point area and took a dirt road toward the river. At the river, they saw an elderly Negro man who looked as if he had lived in the area for a long, long time. They described the house to him and asked if he knew where it was.

"You must be huntin' the mansion," he said. "It's still out there in the woods, far as I know." And he gave them directions for reaching the place.

The couple parked their car where their informant had directed them to, and they got out to begin their search on foot. They had gone only a short distance when the tops of tall magnolia trees glistening in thickets of cedars and gums indicated that they had found the home site.

They pushed through heavy undergrowth and snarls of vines until they reached a sort of clearing—and there it was.

Looming up before them was a house grander than any they had ever imagined. Even with its sagging shutters and drab walls and with its unchecked growth of strangling vegetation, the house had dignity and a touching air of defiance.

The house looked as if it had been waiting for Mr. and Mrs. Snow to rescue it.

After the couple had purchased the house (there was never any doubt that if they possibly could they would find the owners and would buy Waverley) in 1962, they and their three children hacked a path from the road to the house and moved in.

For the first time since 1913, Waverley was occupied.

During the nearly half-century that the grand old place stood vacant, ghostly legends flourished about Waverley. Nocturnal visitors told of hearing the sounds of sprightly music and laughter and dancing feet in the long-deserted house. Others told of seeing a kaleidoscope of faces in the tall, dusty mirrors in the stairwell, faces, perhaps, of people who had paused to gaze into those mirrors long ago and whose reflections were eternally etched on the silvery surfaces.

There were accounts, too, of sightings of a ghostly Indian riding a loping horse across the prairie near Waverley.

The Snows, when they heard such stories, listened with interest, just as they listened to all stories about Waverley and its former occupants. They understood that such a house as theirs almost demanded the presence of ghosts, and they realized that it would have been considered an affront, a deliberate insult by the spirit world, if Waverley had not been properly haunted.

They even decided who some of the ghosts might be, giving them names and identities.

The Indian, of course, was Major John Pytchlyn, Sr., who really was not an Indian at all though most people thought he was. Pytchlyn, the orphan son of an English officer, was reared by the Choctaws and adopted their customs.

He grew to be a wealthy and influential man, and when he died in 1835, many men of prominence attended his funeral rites near the present site of Waverley.

In accordance with Choctaw custom, Pytchlyn's war paraphernalia was placed in the coffin with him. His horse, a fine animal which Pytchlyn rode almost daily over the large acreage he owned, was brought to the edge of the grave to be killed and buried with his owner. At this point in the ritual, Judge Samuel Gholson of Aberdeen interrupted the ceremony to plead for the animal's life.

"It is not necessary to take the life of this fine animal," he said to Pytchlyn's widow. "The Great Spirit already has a gallant mount, a horse worthy of so fine a rider, waiting for our friend in the Happy Hunting Grounds."

The widow was moved by the judge's plea, and she spared the life of the horse.

The ghostly Indian seen near Waverley, the Snows decided, could only be the restless spirit of John Pytchlyn coming back to get his beloved horse and ride him to the Happy Hunting Grounds.

Sometimes they played a game of trying to guess whose ghostly images would be caught in the mirrors at Waverley.

One of the reflections would, of course, certainly be that of Colonel Young himself, Colonel George Hampton Young, the builder of Waverley. Thought he was not a vain man, Colonel Young must have looked at himself with pride. Any man would be proud of Waverley and of the family Colonel Young reared there.

The Colonel, a native of Oglethorpe County, Georgia, came to Mississippi in 1835 to attend the land sales at Pontotoc. He liked what he saw, and he stayed. He had practiced law in Georgia and had served in the state legislature (he studied law at Georgia's Franklin College and at Columbia College in New York), but land development claimed his interest in Mississippi.

He first settled on a farm near West Point on what was known as Colbert Prairies. The land bore the name of James Colbert, a white settler among the Chickasaws, from whom Colonel Young bought five sections of land. Later he purchased land at Mullen's Bluff on the Tombigbee River where he established a permanent home for his family.

It was here, to Waverley, that Mrs. Young brought boxwood plants from her beloved Georgia. She and her children and the boxwood plants joustled in a wagon from Georgia, across northern Alabama to their new home in "the Mississippi wilderness."

The aristocratic boxwood, Mrs. Young felt, were appropriate reminders of the family's sentimental and cultural ties with Georgia. They somehow symbolized a way of life dear to her, so she cared for the plants during the tiring journey almost as carefully as she tended her children.

Mrs. Young planted her boxwood in the prairie soil, but she never saw the beauty they lent to the landscaping of Waverley: she died before that grand house was completed.

The boxwood still thrive at Waverley where visitors marvel at their size. The plants have grotesque shapes though, having been pruned by generations of deer munching on their branches. Mrs. Young would never have approved!

The children grew up at Waverley, the six sons and four daughters, and several of them were married there. Colonel Young had prepared for those weddings when he planned Waverley: the parlor contains an arched alcove, outlined with decorative plastering, designated as the "wedding alcove," and here the bridal couples stood for their wedding ceremonies.

The imaginative and progressive master of Waverley incorporated other luxurious features into his home. The chandeliers were lighted with gas which he manufactured by burning fat pine knots in a retort near the house. There were bathtubs big enough for leisurely soaking, and, for summer use, there was a brick and marble swimming pool at the foot of a gentle hill.

There were also an ice house, a cotton gin, a tannery, a sawmill, a grist mill, a brick kiln, orchards, vineyards, stables, gardens, kennels, warehouses, a boat house, and a ferry. Waverley was almost a self-contained fiefdom.

No one could fault the creator of such an estate if he paused to admire himself in the mirror. Colonel Young's face

109

would logically be one of the fleeting, changing montage of images glimpsed in the mirror The Snows tried to name others who had interrupted walks across the ballroom to gaze at their reflections in the mirrors.

Who were they? Guests at balls, their names long forgotten...Soldiers—six of them bearing the proud name of Young—resplendent in their Confederate uniforms... Politicians come to discuss current topics with Colonel Young...Artisans and scholars...Plantation musicians and traveling preachers...Servants and overseers...They all left their mark on Waverley.

The sounds of revelry that reportedly came from the long-empty house could also be accounted for. With a family of four beautiful daughters and six handsome sons, Waverley's master delighted in hosting parties and balls for them. On many nights, hundreds of couples danced beneath the cupola in the great rotunda, guests of the genial and hospitable Colonel Young. Surely such sounds of gaiety and music would hover about Waverley, clamoring to be heard again.

Though they found it entertaining to try to account for and identify the ghosts they had inherited—if indeed the legends were true—Mr. and Mrs. Snow still cannot explain some of the strange things that happened to them after they moved to Waverley.

Their move was hurried. News of the purchase of the plantation manor attracted curiosity seekers, not all of them desirable or trustworthy, and Mr. and Mrs. Snow moved their family to Waverley earlier than they had planned to protect the structure from pillage.

During the forty-nine years that Waverley stood vacant, vandals did little damage to it. Only three of the more than seven hundred walnut spindles outlining the stairs and the balconies were missing, and only one of the Venetian glass sidelights was broken. Mirrors, chandeliers, carpets, orna-

110

mental plasterings, and brass cornices remained undisturbed, just as the final Young resident had left them. Intruders respected Waverley too much to destroy it.

Living conditions were rather primitive the first few months after the Snows began their restoration of Waverley. There was no electricity, and there was no water either. During those early months, life for the Snows was much more difficult than it had ever been for members of the Young family.

One night, the first week they moved into Waverley, the entire family was awakened by what sounded like an explosion in or quite near the house. The Snows snatched flashlights and made a hurried search of the premises to find what had blown up and to assess the damage.

They found absolutely nothing that could have caused the startling noise.

A few nights later, the episode was repeated: everybody in the family was awakened by a loud explosion, a search was made, but nothing was found.

These explosive noises continued two or three nights each week during the first year the Snows lived at Waverley. After awhile, they became somewhat accustomed to them and did not get out of bed to go investigate. They would mutter drowsily, "There's that noise again!" and go back to sleep.

"We still wonder about that explosive sound, repeated night after night," Mrs. Snow says. "It sounded like the noise made by slapping a big board or some other wide, flat object down on the surface of water with great force. It was louder than that, but that's the best description I can give of it. It seemed that something, something supernatural perhaps, was objecting to our moving into Waverley. We were never really afraid, but we were annoyed—and puzzled. We still are."

After that first year, the baffling noise was never heard

again.

Some months after the cessation of the nighttime explosions, another presence, a gentle presence, came to Waverley.

Mrs. Snow was walking across the upstairs balcony one day when a child's voice called quite distinctly, "Mama. Mama!" Mrs. Snow glanced down quickly, half expecting to see a child standing beside her, but no one was there.

It was not the familiar voice of one of her own children, nor did she recognize it as belonging to any child she knew. It was clear and sweet, and it had a memory-stirring quality as if it were calling from a time long past.

That was the first of many occasions when Mrs. Snow heard the child call. Often it seemed that the little girl (Mrs. Snow, though she never saw her, pictured the caller as four or five years old, a dainty little girl with blonde curly hair) followed her as she went about her household tasks, and occasionally she would call, "Mama—Mama," as though to remind her busy mother that she was there.

Several times the child's calls came during the night, waking Mrs. Snow and sending her across the hall to see about her children even though she knew it was not they who had called. Late one night the Snow's daughter, about ten or twelve years old, came into her parents' room and said,

"I heard the little girl calling you. Is she all right?"

Each time she heard the little girl calling for her mama, Mrs. Snow wondered who the phantom child was and who her mother was. Sometimes her heart ached for them, for the sadness of a little girl lost.

There are several small graves in the burying ground near Waverley, but records do not indicate that there were deaths among children in the Young family. All ten of Colonel George Young's children grew to adulthood. Yet Mrs. Snow believed that the voice belonged to a child who was accustomed to being at Waverley, who felt at home there.

The voice could have been that of one of the Young grandchildren who returned to Waverley with her mother to spend the War years there. Or it might have been the voice of a child who came with her family to refugee at Waverley during the tragic months of defeat and reconstruction. Many people accepted Colonel Young's hospitality during that time, and some of them likely brought small children with them.

The spirit of the little girl, whatever her background, most often made herself known by her soft, endearing calls for her mother, but there were other evidences of her presence.

Sometimes, particularly on long summer afternoons, Mrs. Snow found the imprint of a child's body on a freshly-made bed in the upstairs bedroom.

The imprint looked as if a little girl, tired from play, had gone upstairs and had crawled into the high bed to take a nap in the cool quietness of the empty room.

The child's calls and her afternoon naps continued over a period of five years or so. The manifestations of her presence were not made daily or even weekly, but Mrs. Snow missed her when she stayed away long.

One day while she was busy in the kitchen, Mrs. Snow heard the child's voice right beside her. "I thought she would reach up and grab my apron—the voice was that close," she recalls.

For the first time, the child sounded distressed. "Mama—Mama! Mama!!" she called, as though she needed the immediate reassurance of her mother's presence.

"What's wrong?" Mrs. Snow asked aloud. "Do you need anything? You know I will help you if I can." She had never spoken to the spirit before.

There was no reply.

The child's voice has never since been heard at Waverley,

Sometimes Mrs. Snow found the imprint of a child's body on a freshly-made bed in the upstairs bedroom.

and the bed in the upstairs bedroom stays neatly made, its counterpane smooth and unrumpled.

The little girl, the spirit child, is lost.

Errolton built in 1848 in Columbus.

Nellie

Sitting on the front porch of the old Weaver home and rocking and listening to Miss Nellie talk was as fine a history lesson about Columbus as anybody could have.

Miss Nellie knew everything there was to know about that old river town. She knew about the buildings, and she knew about the people whose lives were a part of those buildings.

She also knew nearly everybody who passed along the sidewalk in front of her house, and she interrupted her rocking and her talking to speak to them and to inquire about members of their families. Each passerby stirred another of Miss Nellie's cubbyholes of memories and prompted the telling of another chapter in the chronicles of Columbus.

As she grew older—she lived to be eighty—Miss Nellie spent more and more time in her rocking chair on the front porch. Looking out across the boxwood hedge and the iron fence (both there before she was born) with her back to the cracked windows and the broken shutters and the dingy walls, she could forget for a little while that her house was worn and shabby.

The house seemed to have gone down—that was a term her father would have used—so quickly that she was overwhelmed by the magnitude of the repairs it needed. Yet she knew that was not true: the changes had come gradually. Time and neglect, not wilful neglect but neglect nevertheless, had taken their relentless toll.

She remembered walking through the back parlor one afternoon (was it last year? five years ago? ten?) and glanced into the tall mirror. A stranger, wrinkled and disheveled, stared back at her.

For the first time, Miss Nellie knew that she was old.

Having seen the changes in herself, she looked closely at her house. It, too, had changed: the graceful elegance of the familiar rooms, rooms where she had spent her entire life, had been swallowed up by deterioration and drabness. Going from room to room, Miss Nellie felt like an intruder, as though she had mistakenly come to the wrong address.

"Well," she said aloud, "we've gotten old, this house and I. Not long ago, this was the loveliest house, and I was the prettiest girl in Columbus. But we're quality—we'll survive."

It was true, her observation about the loveliness of the house and her own beauty.

The house had been built by her father, William B. Weaver, a Columbus merchant, in 1848. That was in the prosperous pre-War days when there was money and labor to indulge the tastes of cultured men such as William Weaver for residences of classic elegance.

Select lumber was shipped up the Tombigbee River from Mobile. Marble mantels were imported from Italy. The front of the house had an Italianate influence with its delicate arches of wooden tracery connecting the six octagonal columns. The ceilings were decorated with plaster medallions

118

of acanthus leaves, and flawless pier mirrors reflected the lights from chandeliers into infinity.

It was a lovely house, a perfect setting for a girl as vivacious and as pretty as Nellie Weaver.

Many of the tales Miss Nellie, an older Miss Nellie, told as she rocked on the porch of the old Weaver home were of growing up in that house, of her childhood in Columbus. Her lifetime spanned the years from before the War Between the States to the time of the Great Depression in the 1930s, and her recollections from each period were sharp and delightfully unique.

She told of the night back in 1863—she was eight years old then—when Confederate President Jefferson Davis, who was visiting in Columbus, was awakened by hundreds of voices singing beneath his bedroom window. The townspeople had gathered to serenade their President with Southern airs. President Davis threw a robe over his long nightshirt and came out on a balcony to applaud the music and to make a little speech to the crowd.

"He was visiting in the James Whitfield house—it's the Billups house now—had come to attend a session of the Mississippi Legislature, I think. The capital had been moved here from Jackson. Jefferson Davis wasn't always popular, not even in his native Mississippi, but that night when he stood out there on the balcony with his hair all tousled and his nightshirt flapping around his ankles, the people in Columbus loved him."

She told, too, of the April day in 1866 when the ladies of Columbus (Miss Nellie had not quite attained the status of ladyhood, being only eleven, but she was not one to miss any momentous occasion) marched in a dignified procession to Friendship Cemetery to decorate the graves of the soldiers, Confederate and Union, with fresh flowers from their gardens. It was the first Memorial Day. Miss Nellie remembered

119

how the flowers smelled, the wilted tulle bows that bound some of the bouquets, the sad sameness of the hundreds of earth mounds, and the reluctance of a few of the ladies to put their flowers on Union graves.

When she was older, Miss Nellie attended Columbus Female Institute, and in later years she was frequently called on to supply historic data about this private academy which was, a century and more later, to become Mississippi University for Women.

Growing up during Reconstruction, a time of depression and of re-adjustment, Miss Nellie learned early to adapt to loss and to change. Never in her long life did deprivations or inconveniences dull her keen delight in the wonder of life: for her, every day was a new adventure.

Miss Nellie could make a walk to the Post Office seem as exciting as a New Year's Eve ball. And if a garment needed mending, she could embroider a patch on it and wear it with such verve that every fashionable young lady in Columbus yearned for patches, too.

She had a talent for acting, and she often appeared in amateur theatricals in Columbus. Her portrayal of Lucy in Sheridan's "The Rivals" evoked prolonged applause from the audience at the old Gilmer House, and there were many comments to the effect that "that pretty Weaver girl is wasting her talents here in Columbus." There might have been suggestions that she appear on the New York stage, but the life of a professional actress was not quite acceptable in 1875, not for a Southern lady.

Yellowed clippings tell of her successes in plays and of her popularity at dances and balls. "N. W. was the belle of the Mardi Gras ball," the Columbus society columns reported, printing an observation that everyone at the ball already knew.

Naturally, many young men came calling at the Weaver

home. Miss Nellie enjoyed their company, was pleased with their attention, and graciously accepted their invitations to parties, picnics, boat rides, concerts, dances, parades, and church suppers. She liked them all; no one in particular; all of them.

Then Charles Tucker came to Columbus.

Their meeting was as exciting and as romantic as if it had been written for a story book.

Miss Nellie first saw Charles Tucker—she did not know his name—as he was helping to fight a fierce fire. Probably, like Miss Nellie, he had been attracted to the scene of the fire by curiosity. Once there, he saw that the fire-fighters needed help, so he handed his coat and hat to a stranger and joined in battling the blazes.

That is how Miss Nellie first saw Charles Tucker: his face flushed and streaked with soot, his shirt grimy and wet, his hair wild and disarrayed. In her eyes, he was a dashing hero.

"Who is he?" she asked. "Who is he? He's so handsome! Who is he?"

She must have asked two dozen people before someone told her, "His name is Charles Tucker, and he came from Virginia. Fredericksburg, I think."

Miss Nellie was in love, happily, deliriously, completely in love. She and Charles R. Tucker were married in the First Presbyterian Church in Columbus at 8:30 o'clock on the evening of February 28, 1878.

It may have been about then, either just before or just after she and Charles were married, that Nellie walked into the double parlor at the Weaver house one day and, using her diamond ring, etched NELLIE on a windowpane.

"Now I'll never be forgotten in this house: there will always be this reminder of me here. Always." She stood back and looked at her name on the pane and laughed with delight.

The name stayed on the pane, but the laughter vanished. At least for awhile. Charles and Nellie, they of the storybook romance, did not live happily ever after. They parted, and Miss Nellie reared their daughter, Ellen, in the same big house where she had grown up. Years later, the grandchildren (Nell, Lulah, and the twins, Blanchard and Walter) came to the Weaver home.

For years Miss Nellie taught a private school at her home, earning the money she needed for her livelihood. She converted one of the servants' houses, long empty, in the back yard into a classroom. There she taught the children and the grandchildren of her friends.

Perhaps it was because of her preoccupation with her school and with her grandchildren that Miss Nellie did not notice how disreputable the Weaver place had become. By the time she became aware of it, she had neither the finances nor the energy to restore it.

About this time, about the time she faced and accepted the ravages of age, Miss Nellie's friends intensified their efforts to persuade her to move from the Weaver place into a small apartment or rooms where she would be more comfortable.

At first, Miss Nellie was shocked at their suggestions. Later she became annoyed and stubbornly defensive.

"Leave my home? Never! It needs me, and my grandchildren need me. And I need them. I'll stay right here," she retorted. "Right here." Often she added, "Some day this house will be restored to the beautiful place it once was. You'll see. It will be lovely again."

So Miss Nellie stayed.

She rocked on her porch, and she told stories about the Columbus she loved, and she pretended not to notice that she and her house were both wearing out.

One night Miss Nellie's clothing caught fire from the open fireplace in the back parlor. She died as a result of the burns.

After her death, the Weaver house suffered further at the hands of destructive tenants, and vandals added their indignities to the structure.

Then about 1950, Mrs. Erroldine Hay Bateman bought the property and began its restoration. Her task seemed almost hopeless, but she saw beyond the dingy banners of peeling wallpaper, the cheap partitions that changed grand rooms into makeshift apartments, the leaky roof, and the rotting floors. Mrs. Bateman saw the enduring beauty that William Weaver had built into his house, and she set about to reclaim it.

Mrs. Bateman named the house Errolton.

One day as she and her son, Douglas Bateman, were supervising some basic repairs in the double parlor, they happened to see the windowpane on which Miss Nellie had scratched her name years earlier. Most of the windows had been broken, but the pane with NELLIE on it remained intact.

"We must save that pane," Mrs. Bateman said. "It will be a touching reminder of Miss Nellie and her life in this house."

Unfortunately, a careless workman broke the pane. There was no way to salvage the pieces, so a new pane of glass had to be put in the window.

As the restoration progressed, Errolton became as beautiful as Mrs. Bateman had known it would be. The house seemed to come alive, almost as though it were resurrected, in response to the love and attention given it.

The restoration was nearly finished by the mid-1950s when Mr. and Mrs. Douglas Bateman moved into Errolton. She completed work in the upstairs bedrooms and added her

123

inheritance of fine pieces of furniture to the house.

One afternoon not many years ago, Mrs. Douglas Bateman was walking through the back parlor when she noticed that the sun was shining through the window and was striking a sofa she had recently upholstered in blue. She did not want the sunlight to fade her sofa, so she went over to the window to pull the shade down.

As she reached for the shade, Mrs. Bateman noticed what appeared to be dust on the windowpane. She ran her hand across it, and the glass felt rough. Stepping back, she looked at the pane and saw etched there the word

NELLIE

The word occupied the same position on the pane and in the window as the autographed pane that had been destroyed by the careless workman.

The Batemans think Miss Nellie came back and scratched her name on the windowpane to thank them for making her house lovely again. They call it "Miss Nellie's Window."

Featherston Place in Holly Springs was built in 1834.

The Cameo

Southern folklore provides many methods for keeping evil spirits out of a house or for exorcising such evil spirits as may already be there.

For instance, a horseshoe wrapped in red paper or red cloth and hung, open end down, over the front door will keep evil out. So will three mistletoe seeds placed above the inside door facing. Evil spirits will not enter a house that has its doors and windows painted blue, nor will they go in where a fire is kept burning on the hearth day and night, winter and summer.

A line of salt (plain, not iodized) sprinkled around the house will keep evil spirits out (moats serve the same purpose but it is easier to sprinkle salt than to dig moats), and so will a holly bush planted by the front door.

Bottle trees, made by slipping empty bottles (preferably blue ones) over a tree's limbs, are popular in some places for keeping evil away, and there are other folks who declare there is nothing like having a frizzled chicken scratching around in the yard to "disencourage" unwanted spirits.

There are other things a person can do to give protection from evil—many families have a sort of private potion that works well for them—but these are fairly basic and reliable procedures.

It is doubtful that the late Mrs. George M. Buchanan ever tried any of these old folk methods for ridding her premises of unwanted spirits though she was troubled by a restless ghost in her house in Holly Springs for a long time.

As members of her family recall the story, Mrs. Buchanan had her sleep disturbed night after night by the heavy footsteps of an intruder stamping up the stairs.

The first few times she heard the noise, Mrs. Buchanan was afraid a burglar or some other such undesirable person had broken into her house, though she wondered why any self-respecting thief would be so noisy. Her reading of detective stories and such had led her to believe that burglars, proper ones, crept stealthily about. Certainly they never clumped and stamped as noisily as the one in her house did.

To begin with, she could not decide whether to reprimand the bumpy burglar for breaking tradition, to call the police, or to pretend to be asleep. She was, to tell the truth, a bit frightened: she did not like to have strangers rummaging around unsupervised in her home.

The sensible thing to do, she decided, was to get up and go see what was happening on her stairs. So she did. However, her investigation failed to disclose any intruder—living variety—in the house. Yet Mrs. Buchanan was certain that she had heard heavy footsteps on the stairs.

When the same noise awakened her the next night, she again investigated and again found nothing. It did not take Mrs. Buchanan many nights to decide that it was not a real burglar who was stomping up the steps: she was sure it was a ghost.

Mrs. Buchanan was much less afraid of ghosts than she was of lawless human beings. After a time, she reached a point where she accepted the presence, unwanted though it was, and could even speak casually about having a ghost in her home, Featherston Place.

She wondered occasionally who the ghost might be (Featherston Place was built in 1834, so there were many possibilities), but her principal complaint was a peculiar habit her ghost had.

Night after night Mrs. Buchanan was awakened by the sound of the ghost tromping up the broad wooden stairs. Trouble was, he would go only halfway up the stairs, and then he would stop. There would not be another sound. Nothing.

Mrs. Buchanan would lie in the dark, wide awake, listening for the heavy-footed ghost to complete his journey up the stairs. She could not go back to sleep when she was waiting tensely to hear the footsteps continue. It was like the old gag about waiting for the man upstairs to drop his other shoe. Except that waiting for a ghost to finish going upstairs, Mrs. Buchanan always said, was worse, more nerve-wracking.

Those nights of having her sleep interrupted began to tell on Mrs. Buchanan. She became edgy and a bit irritable (very unlike her), and she knew she had to do something about her halfway-up-the-stairs ghost.

Living in Holly Springs as she did, Mrs. Buchanan had access to an amazingly wide variety of information and advice on exorcising ghosts, including the suggestions offered earlier. She may have considered some of these, but she seems to have rejected them, for one reason or another, in toto.

Finally a course of action came to her during one of those stretches of sleeplessness when she lay in the darkness waiting to hear the steps continue up the stairs.

The next day, she had her stairs carpeted.

Never again did she hear ghostly footsteps go halfway up the stairs. Never again did she lie awake waiting for the steps to continue to the top.

Mrs. Buchanan was delighted with her solution. And she hoped it did not disconcert her stair-climbing ghost.

The ghost of the carpeted stair was not the only spirit at Featherston Place. There were other haunters, noiseless wraiths who wandered about the old house and had encounters with various occupants.

Back in the late 1920s, during the boom years when everybody had money or credit or both, a highly respected professional man (some people said he was connected with a Memphis bank) came to Holly Springs to transact business with the Buchanan family. He accepted their invitation to spend the night at Featherston Place not only because he found the family members to be delightful company but also because the architecture and the history of Featherston Place interested him.

The house, he was told, was built in the 1830s by Alexander McEwen, a merchant who came to Holly Springs from Tennessee. McEwen was credited with giving the town its name: he sent instructions that goods were to be shipped to him at "the holly springs," a well-known landmark among pioneers in north Mississippi, and the name stuck.

The merchant built a modified raised cottage type residence with the dining room, kitchen, and servants' quarters in the exposed basement and the bedrooms and parlor on the first floor.

The house had been restored in 1917, about ten years before the businessman's visit, and he was eager to see how the architect (Theodore C. Link of St. Louis) handled the assignment.

Featherston Place was as charming as the guest had known it would be, and the conversation complemented the setting. It was a fine evening.

The supper menu had featured ham, quite salty, and the guest was thirsty all evening. After he had retired to his room, he kept wishing that he had brought a tall glass of water into the bedroom with him. He was very thirsty. The more he tried to push the thought from his mind, the thirstier he became.

His room did not have a private bath, and he hesitated to go down the hall to the bathroom there for fear he might disturb members of the family. So he tried harder to ignore his thirst and to go to sleep. He tried counting sheep, but his sheep stampeded toward a cool, refreshing meadow pool where they drank and drank and drank. He envied every imaginary sheep.

Sometime after midnight, he did doze off to sleep, but he was tormented by dreams of being lost in a parching desert, and he waked thirstier than ever.

There was nothing to do, he decided, but to tiptoe

down the hall to the bathroom and get a drink of water. He opened his bedroom door quietly and glanced into the hall. His thoughtful host had left a light burning in the bathroom and had left the door slightly ajar so that there was a soft light in the hall.

The guest was just about to step out of his room when he saw an attractive young woman in the hall. Not wishing to frighten or embarrass her, he closed his door and waited several minutes.

After what he considered a decently long wait, he again started out of his room toward the bathroom. The young lady was still in the hall, obviously heading for the same destination.

Again the gentleman closed his door and waited. His thirst by this time was almost unbearable, but he was distracted somewhat by his curiosity as to who the lady in the hall could be. He had not seen her at supper, and there had been no mention of anyone who fit her description. Her presence puzzled him.

His great thirst, growing more intense by the minute, prompted him to open the door again. When he looked out, the young woman was still in the hall. This time, however, the guest decided that he had been patient and gentlemanly long enough, so he left his room and walked down the hall. As he brushed past the lady, he murmured, "Pardon me, please," and continued on his mission.

She made no reply, and when, his thirst assuaged, he came out of the bathroom, she was no longer in the hall.

The entire episode was strange, but he was too sleepy to lie awake thinking about it.

Next morning at breakfast, he expected to see the young woman he had encountered in the hall, but she was not at the table. He made discreet inquiries about other guests in the house or other members of the family whom he had not met, but he learned nothing. Finally curiosity prompted him to discard mannerly restraint and to ask who the roamer was.

"I—I," he began hesitantly, "saw a young lady in the upstairs hall last night. I spoke to her, but she did not reply, and I wondered—well, I do want to know who she was!"

The members of the family exchanged quick glances, and one of them replied, "You have seen our ghost. Frankly, we do not know who she is, but she appears here at Featherston Place every now and then. She didn't frighten you, did she?"

"No. I wasn't frightened. Actually it never occurred to me that I was seeing a ghost or I might have been afraid. I just wondered who she was and why she kept standing out in the hall."

"So do we," his hosts answered.

Though they do not know who the young ghost is, the

occupants of Featherston Place have established the identity of another female ghost, an older woman, who has appeared there through the years.

This apparition roams about the house and grounds as though she is completely at home and as though she might be making certain that the property is being properly cared for.

When she first appeared, fifty years or more ago, people who saw her—and many people did—all gave similar descriptions of her appearance. She was old, they said, and was dressed in dark clothing. She had a shawl around her stooped shoulders, and she wore a large cameo brooch.

Among the people who saw the elderly ghost was a young mother from Memphis who had brought her baby to Holly Springs for a visit. This was in the late 1930s.

The mother and baby were occupying the guest room at Featherston Place. The baby had been restless, probably because of being in a new place, and had kept the mother awake later than usual. When the child finally went to sleep, the mother left a night light burning in the room in case she needed to see about the wakeful baby again.

They were both asleep when the mother aroused suddenly with the feeling that someone was in the room with them.

She sat up in bed and looked over to make sure her baby was all right. She saw a woman leaning over the baby's cradle and holding out her arms as if she were about to pick up the infant.

The mother screamed.

The figure at the cradle vanished instantly, disappeared into thin air.

Later, when she was calmer, the mother described the ghost she had seen. She, too, told of the shawl and of the cameo.

It was the brooch—the cameo—which provided the clue to

the ghost's identity. As members of the family began seeking
out older residents of Holly Springs to ask their help in iden-
tifying the phantom, they went one day to the home of a
blacksmith, a man long retired from active work in his trade.

He listened as the ghost was described to him, and he
shook his head until his caller described the cameo. Then he
exclaimed,

"That's Mrs. McEwen! She wore that big carved pin all

the time. Everybody who ever saw her would know her by that pin." He paused. "I guess I'm the only one left in Holly Springs who ever saw Mrs. McEwen or that pin.

"I was a young man—a long time ago—and I was doing some blacksmith work for her son-in-law, General Winfield Scott Featherston. He was a fine man, General Featherston. He and his wife were living at Featherston Place, and Mrs. McEwen was living with them. I used to see her walking around like she was supervising the place.

"The servants didn't like her much, said she was bossy. That's natural, I guess. She and her husband had built the house, you know, right after they came to Holly Springs, and she must have felt like she should still be in charge of it all.

"She used to say wasn't anybody going to run her out of her own house. Not that anybody ever tried to or wanted to, far as I know. She was getting real old—Lord! I thought she was the oldest woman in the world then, but I don't expect she was as old as I am now—and sort of peculiar maybe.

"Anyhow, she used to talk about how she wasn't ever going to leave her house. Not ever.

"Well, this time I started telling about, I was doing a little work for General Featherston. Mrs. McEwen came out on the porch and called me. Said she had broken the catch on her cameo (don't know that I had ever heard that word before) and wanted me to fix it for her.

"I wasn't used to doing little tedious jobs like that, but her being old and I could tell she was real upset about breaking her pin and all, I told her I'd try to fix it. And I did.

"She told me then she was going to stay at her house (seemed like she didn't ever call it Featherston Place) forever and that she was going to wear that cameo the longest day she was in this world.

"That's what she said. And she's still wandering around

Featherston Place and still wearing that cameo pin, from what you say.

"I must have fixed it real good!"

Old Mathis plantation site near Pope.

That Black Cat

To tell the truth, there was not a whole lot of grieving in Panola County when George Mathis died. Some folks said the preacher sat up all night trying to think of something good to say about him at the funeral service. He, the preacher, finally ended up just reading some Scripture and praying for the family of the deceased, which was about the best anybody could do under the circumstances.

At the graveyard, while the dirt was being shoveled over the coffin, one of George Mathis' neighbors said louder than he intended to, "That's sure one man who is going as straight to hell as a martin to his gourd." Everybody standing around the graveyard heard him say it, and it sort of shocked them, him saying it right out in front of everybody and all, but nobody denied it. In fact, it sounded like several "Amens" were said. Subdued ones, of course.

That remark would not have upset old George Mathis one whit, would not have bothered him at all. He had been threatened with hell fire since his streak of meanness started showing, which was about the time he was half grown, but he would laugh a mean laugh and say he did not believe in such.

He did not believe in anything except work, and there was never a man—or a woman—who could work hard enough or long enough or good enough to please him. He would set tasks for his field hands that no plain human beings could get done, and then he would rave and rant and carry on when the hands did not do what he had told them to do. He would deal out right harsh punishment too, folks said. It was said that Mathis had flailed a good many men with a scantling when they displeased him, and a good many men bore permanent marks of Mathis' displeasure.

He would put folks off his land, too, turn them out of the shabby tenant houses that dotted his plantation any time he took a notion. At least that was the reputation he had. It did not bother him a bit, folks said, if his tenants had nowhere to move or if the weather was miserable (seems most of his tenants were put off during cold, rainy spells) or if they had no way to carry the little shirttail full of things they owned. When George Mathis said, "Go!" he meant go. Right then.

Mathis, if folks remember right, mistreated his own family. They were scared of his wild tantrums, and they tried to stay out of his way.

So far as anybody can recollect, George Mathis never said a kind or a pleasant word to anybody.

He was a fractious man.

Well, they say that one cold winter day Mathis had a run-in with one of his tenants, an old black everybody called Bo-Man.

Bo-Man grew up in Louisiana (his name was likely Beau Man there), but he had lived in Panola County so long most folks forgot he had ever lived anywhere else. Bo-Man farmed on the Mathis land longer than anybody else ever had, but one day he got his back hurt while he was clearing new ground. He was pretty stove up from the accident, and when

George Mathis saw that Bo-Man would likely be no account for a long time, he told him to get his family and his things off the place.

Bo-Man did not think Mr. Mathis was doing him right, and he made bold to tell him so. He told Mr. Mathis that he was an old man and that his back hurt so bad he just could put one foot in front of the other one, and that his wife was sick, and that they did not have even a shed or a stable they could move into, and that he did not have a crying penny to his name.

None of that made any difference to George Mathis.

"Get off my land right now!" he shouted at Bo-Man. He picked up a limb in the yard and started toward Bo-Man with it, but Bo-Man dodged and jumped through the door (seems like he forgot about his ailing back for a minute) and slammed it shut and bolted it.

Mathis stomped around the porch, beating on the door and the shutters and the wall with his stick and hollering at Bo-Man. He talked right rough.

Bo-Man answered him slow and plain from inside the house. "I'll leave, but you'll wish you hadn't run me off. I will put a spell on you and on this place so nobody will ever forget this day."

That kind of talk really made Mathis mad. He fumed and bellowed and even threatened to burn the house down with Bo-Man inside, but finally he left.

Bo-Man had learned some voodoo when he lived down in Louisiana, and maybe he did and maybe he did not put a spell on George Mathis and on the place. Strange things began to happen though, bad things.

First off, George Mathis took sick and died. Nobody ever knew exactly what ailed him: it just seemed like he choked to death.

Somebody said a conjure ball was found under George

Mathis' front steps. Somebody else told about finding a little mud doll by the path back of the Mathis house. The doll was real plain, sort of a stick doll made out of red clay. Even though it was crude, the doll looked sort of like Mathis: it had a frown, a turned-down mouth and mean little eyes.

There was a cotton string tied real tight around the doll's neck.

Well, when the church bell tolled the news that George Mathis had died, neighbors began to gather, the way they always do. The men nailed together some heavy pine boards they found out in the barn and made a coffin for Mathis. They dug the grave, too, and they washed him and put his Sunday clothes on him. The washing and the dressing they did before they made the coffin or dug the grave. That always came first.

It was early evening, dusky dark, when they finished everything. They put George Mathis' body in the coffin, and they toted the coffin into the parlor. Somebody had brought sawhorses, and the men sat the coffin on them. The saw-horses should have had a black cover over them, to sort of hide what they were, but nobody covered those sawhorses that held George Mathis' coffin. They just did not. It was like the neighbors would do what they absolutely had to do but nothing else.

One of the things they felt obliged to do was sit up with the corpse. There was a feeling that the Bible said neighbors should sit up with the dead even though nobody could name the chapter and verse where the admonition was found.

So the neighbors—a good many of them—sat up. They sat in the parlor, solemn and uncomfortable, the way folks are around the dead.

All of a sudden an awful racket commenced. It sounded like every dog in the country had set up a steady howl. They howled and they howled and they howled. Dogs came loping from every direction to join in the loud tuneless chorus.

Every man at the house tried to shut the dogs up and chase them away, but they could not do either. The howling kept up until, like they had got a signal of some kind, the dogs got as quiet as rotten stumps. Then they slowly circled the house, running around and around without making a sound.

Somehow the silence was worse than the howling had been.

After several laps around the house, the whole pack of dogs chased off across the fields.

The men went back inside. They did not talk about the way the dogs had acted. They did not know what to say.

Some of them yawned: it was a good bit past bedtime. "It will be a long night," one of the men said, "a long night." He stood up and stretched and scratched the back of his neck.

Just then a big black cat came into the room and began circling around and around the coffin, squalling and caterwaulling.

"Scat!" a woman said. "Get out of here! You're making enough fuss to wake the dead!"

Then she was embarrassed by what she had said, and she left the room.

The cat did not leave though. He just kept on walking around and around the coffin, taking his time, and yelling louder on every round.

"Out!" two of the men started toward the cat, and one of them kicked him. He did not really kick the cat though: the cat disappeared before the man's foot touched him. That man's foot just swung through thin air.

Folks looked at each other. Then they looked all around the room. The doors and windows were all shut, but the cat was gone.

A big black cat came into the room and began circling around.

The watchers did not have long to wonder about this turn of events because in a few minutes the cat was back, patroling around George Mathis' coffin again. He stopped every now and then to arch his back and rub up against the sawhorses. Then he would sharpen his claws on the bare wood. He never stopped howling.

That cat raised such a ruckus the watchers could not hear each other shouting, "Scat!" and, "Get out!" and, "Hush your fuss!"

A woman picked up a broom and started swinging it at the cat.

The cat disappeared. Vanished into nothingness.

The watchers were just settling down again when the cat came back. He took up his noisesome route around the corpse just like he never had left.

It kept up like that all night: every time the black cat was chased away, he would come back to yowl around the coffin again.

The watchers were mighty glad when daylight came.

After the funeral service, a day or so afterwards, George Mathis' son Sid was walking across the yard toward the fields with Uncle Jake, a former slave who had come back to pay his respects to the family.

"Mister Sid," Uncle Jake said, "don't you hear Mister George calling you? Seems like I been hearing your pa call you ever since I got here."

Sid was glad—more relieved than glad, really—when Uncle Jake spoke like that. Ever since Sid had come back home from the graveyard, he had heard his father calling him. At first it had been just a whisper, but it got louder and louder all the time. "Sid! Sid!! Sid!!!"

Sid thought he might be going crazy. Nobody else heard George Mathis' voice, just Sid, until Uncle Jake heard it.

But even the comfort of knowing that Uncle Jake heard

the voice too did not blot it out. The familiar voice kept calling Sid louder and louder until he could not stand it any longer.

Sid turned the place over to a cousin, Ben Hentz, and left.

But even after Sid left, unsettling things kept happening at the Mathis place.

Late every afternoon, along about first dark, all the dogs would bristle up and snarl like they saw something fearsome coming at them. Then the whole pack of them would circle around the house and head out across the fields. They would yelp and bay like they were trailing something. Whatever it was, only the dogs could see it.

They would come back hours later, plumb worn out and acting sort of like they were in a trance.

Then next day the dogs would carry on the same way again. Every afternoon they went tearing off after something nobody could see.

There were other unnatural goings-on. Beginning the night after George Mathis died, folks in the house heard loud knockings and scratchings at the doors, like somebody—or something—was having a frantic fit to get in. But when they opened the door, there never was anybody—or anything—there.

Then there were the dreadful nights when every member of the household was waked by the rumbling sound of empty barrels rolling down the wide hall and crashing into the walls. It was a terrifying noise, but nobody ever found where it came from. Though dozens of people were roused from sound sleep by the thunder of rolling barrels (they all said the rumbling was made by empty barrels turning over real fast), no one could find a barrel or even a keg that could have made the blam-blam-blam noise in the hall.

A few times when the men were hunting for the phantom barrels, they met a strange black cat sauntering down the hall. They said the cat stared at them with evil eyes.

Not all the unnerving happenings took place at night. Often during the broad open daylight after the women folks had made up the beds all neat and nice, they would go back into the bedrooms and find the covers all tumbled and tangled. The beds looked like somebody had thrashed about during a terrible nightmare or maybe that there had been a knock-down-drag-out fight. The feather pillows, plumped up and smooth a few minutes before, had deep dents in them, the kind a troubled head would make.

It was not long before Ben Hentz and his family moved off the place. Nobody blamed them.

Other tenants came and went. Not any of them stayed long. They could not stand the yapping dogs or the strange scratchings or the blamming barrels or the tousled beds. A monstrous big black cat bothered them, too. So they left.

The house stood empty a long time. Now a pile of rotting timbers and a broken chimney mark the place.

Occasionally folks tell about seeing a black cat stalk out of the crumbling chimney. They say the cat has a self-satisfied smirk and that he strolls around the ruined house with a proud air like he owns the property.

Afterword to the Commemorative Edition

In the mid-1960s—maybe because she had publishing friends in north Alabama, or maybe because she thought it would sell and she sure could use the money, or maybe just because she wanted to see if she was up to the challenge—Mother decided she would write a cookbook. *Treasured Alabama Recipes* became an instant big seller, largely because of the stories that accompanied the family collection of recipes.

Shortly after the release of the cookbook, Margaret Gillis Figh, one of Mother's college English professors, called her. "Kathryn, you are going to write another book, and this time it doesn't need to have any recipes in it. It needs to be a book of stories," Dr. Figh told her. "I'll be your collaborator if you like."

About this same time unexplained occurrences began in our house.

I was the only child still at home, my older sister and brother by then off at college. One afternoon Mother and I were in the kitchen rolling out cookie dough. Our house was small but big enough. The narrow kitchen immediately adjoined the small dining room, which opened through paned double doors into the living room.

That afternoon is indelibly imprinted in my memory. I'd floured the rolling pin and Mother had dampened the counter so the edges of the waxed paper wouldn't roll up. We'd sprinkled more flour on the waxed paper—when making cookies nothing should stick to anything else—and the lump of dough was plopped down and ready to roll out.

At that very moment we heard a ruckus in the living room unlike anything I've ever heard since: loud and scratching noises that seemed to come from not one particular area of the room, but rather from a room filled completely with the unsettling sound as though the midget demons of hell might have been turned loose all at once.

We looked at each other, startled, and moved to investigate. Mother wiped flour on her apron as she hurried to open the double doors into the living room. At the first movement of the doors the room became totally silent—no, eerily silent. I was right beside my mother, looking through the panes into the room. "What was that, Mama?" I asked her more out of curiosity than fear. She hesitated. "I have no earthly idea," she said finally.

We stood there for a minute before Mother dismissed it as a squirrel that might have fallen down into the fireplace, though there was no squirrel. There was nothing in that room except the furniture. We went back into the kitchen. As soon as the dough was almost thin enough to make acceptably crisp cookies, it began again, this time louder and with more force than before. And again, the minute Mother pushed the door, it all stopped. Not one item in the room was disturbed. Not one picture was crooked. Not one glass paperweight had fallen from the mantel.

Though Mother and I waited with some anticipation, the remainder of that day was quiet, ordinary. But in the weeks and months that followed, the unaccountable goings-on continued. They began with loud footsteps clumping down the hall, the steps ending abruptly just inside my brother's bedroom with a jarring slam of the door.

Subsequent strangeness took the form of furniture rearranging, not just shifting a bit as it would if a foundation was settling, but honest-to-goodness interior redecorating—beds rearranged to balance dressers moved from one wall to another. Freshly baked cakes flying—not falling, but *sailing*—off the dining room table. We were amazed, entertained, puzzled, but we were never frightened. My brother and sister pooh-poo-hed our stories on their first visits home from college. But as the unusual goings-on manifested themselves to my siblings, they, too, were intrigued.

DILCY WINDHAM HILLEY

∽

My mother was a multifaceted woman.

She taught a Sunday school class and made sure we went to church twice on the Sabbath. She was a believer.

She also was generous, perhaps to a fault. One Christmas we got extra stockings. As always, we drove down later to my grandmother's house in Thomasville, but Mother made an unexpected detour down a dirt road that she chose at random. We saw an African American woman walking with two small children. They were total strangers to us.

Mother stopped the car and asked me to give the children our extra stockings that were filled with candy, toys, and fruit. The children's mother's eyes sparkled.

"Santa Claus has come for you at the store and now he's come here," she told the children.

That was so like Mother. She told me about visiting a poor family with her father, who was a country banker, when she was young. She played in the dirt with the family's children that afternoon, and later she and her father shared in their meager evening meal.

"You're not better than they are," her father told her when they left. "You're just used to better things." She remembered the lesson all her life.

On the other hand, she believed in the supernatural.

I was skeptical of Jeffrey and her stories. Whenever someone asked me if I believed, my stock reply was, "Sure! Jeffrey sent me to college."

That always drew a laugh from the visitor and a wry smile from Mother.

One day, I was preparing to leave Selma for a job in New Mexico. My suitcase was packed and on my bed. Knowing that I had a long way to drive and that it would be many months before I saw Mother again, I embraced her in a lengthy good-bye hug.

Suddenly, my suitcase jumped from my bed, flipped over twice in the air, and landed beside me.

Mother and I just stared at each other.

"Jeffrey," she finally whispered. She wore the same wry smile.

I hit the road quickly. After that, I, too, was a believer.

BEN WINDHAM